Intruder!

On one of the cameras he'd set up while Alyssa had been in the shower last night, Blake saw a hooded figure move through the garage.

Intruder.

A second alarm sounded. There were at least two people breeching the house. He checked the second camera that he'd set up at the front door. Blake moved to the closet and traded his Colt for a shotgun. He dialed 911, thinking he was grateful to live so close to his station.

"Alyssa, wake up. We have intruders."

She startled awake, sitting up and rubbing her eyes. Her sleepy look tugged at his heart.

"Dispatch, what's your emergency?"

"This is Officer Blake O'Connor. Two men are breaking into my house. I need immediate assistance." He tossed the phone onto the bed and then helped Alyssa. Going downstairs was out of the question. The only option was to head up.

"Come on," he said quietly, looking into her huge blue eyes.

He needed to secure her in the attic...so he could confront the intruders.

TEXAS BABY CONSPIRACY

USA TODAY Bestselling Author

BARB HAN

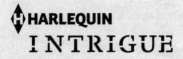

HARLEQUIN

INTRIGUE

All my love to Brandon, Jacob and Tori, the three great loves of my life.

To Babe, my hero, for being my best friend, greatest love and my place to call home.

I love you all with everything that I am.

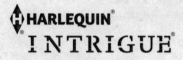

Recycling programs for this product may not exist in your area.

ISBN-13: 978-1-335-48915-9

Texas Baby Conspiracy

Copyright © 2021 by Barb Han

This edition published by arrangement with Harlequin Books S.A.

For questions and comments about the quality of this book, please contact us at CustomerService@Harlequin.com.

Harlequin Enterprises ULC
22 Adelaide St. West, 40th Floor
Toronto, Ontario M5H 4E3, Canada
www.Harlequin.com

Printed in U.S.A.

USA TODAY bestselling author **Barb Han** lives in north Texas with her very own hero-worthy husband, three beautiful children, a spunky golden retriever/standard poodle mix and too many books in her to-read pile. In her downtime, she plays video games and spends much of her time on or around a basketball court. She loves interacting with readers and is grateful for their support. You can reach her at barbhan.com.

Books by Barb Han

Harlequin Intrigue

An O'Connor Family Mystery

Texas Kidnapping
Texas Target
Texas Law
Texas Baby Conspiracy

Rushing Creek Crime Spree

Cornered at Christmas
Ransom at Christmas
Ambushed at Christmas
What She Did
What She Knew
What She Saw

Decoding a Criminal

Visit the Author Profile page at Harlequin.com.

CAST OF CHARACTERS

Alyssa Hazel (O'Connor)—She can't remember much of anything except loving the one man she seems to have pushed away.

Blake O'Connor—This Houston beat cop never stopped loving the woman who sent him divorce papers and will do whatever it takes to protect her.

Liz Roark—This officer was close with Blake on the job... Was she too close?

Gruff—He might not want to hurt Alyssa because she has a kid on the way, but how far will he go to get information out of her?

Nasal—He has a job to do and doesn't care how pregnant Alyssa is.

Bus Stop—Is he behind the abduction or a pawn?

The Judge—Is he a real judge or does he consider himself judge and jury?

Chapter One

When Alyssa Hazel stirred and felt nothing but walls on all four sides of her, shock robbed her voice. Panic caused her pulse to pound and the extra blood thumped against her skull. Her head threatened to split open as she tried to recall where she was and why she was here.

She pushed her hands out, trying to see if the walls would give. The material was pliable but solid enough to hold form. She felt for cracks or anything she could grip. Movement hurt. She attempted to stretch out her legs and couldn't get very far.

Where was she? What happened? Why was she enclosed in such a tight space? A haze pressed down on her brain and the pressure was the equivalent of a thunderstorm rolling in.

It was pitch black and she couldn't remember a thing about where she'd been or what she'd been doing before ending up in this…whatever *this* was. Forcing recall only made her brain hurt more. A stomach cramp drew her legs tighter to her belly.

Wouldn't there be a door if she was in some kind of compartment? There would have to be a crack around a door or hatch. She reached up and couldn't find a ceiling. That seemed like the first good sign so far. It meant that she might be in a small closet or storage room.

She felt around, trying to get her bearings because right now she was at a loss as to where she was and what she was doing there. Bringing her hands to cradle her stomach, she knew one thing was certain, she was pregnant. Very pregnant. Her belly was huge.

Again, her mind drew a blank to a question that was so basic she felt like she should have an answer. What on earth was she doing there? She brought her hand up to her head and looked for a reason for the memory loss and headache. She touched a tender spot and felt dried blood.

At least she thought it was. Seeing was impossible despite her eyes adjusting to the dark.

Logic said if she'd gotten inside this structure, there had to be a way out. Bracing her hands against thin walls, she maneuvered up to a sitting position.

Next, she instinctively checked to make sure she had on clothes and then immediately checked for her wedding ring. The band was gone. Thank heavens she had on a cotton shirt and jeans. No shoes but she did have on socks. She remembered wearing her favorite boots. The random memory seemed to float around with no context to ground it. Where had she been going? What had she been doing?

A noise startled her. She froze, unable to make out what it was or exactly where it came from other than *out there*.

There had to be a handle or lock that she could maneuver in order to free herself. But when she ran her hand along the fiberglass, she felt nothing but a hole where a knob should be. She ran her fingers over it and through it, trying to figure out how to open it. Then, she realized it was a pocket door.

The door slid open easily once she figured out how it worked. Light practically blinded her. She brought her hand up to shield her eyes from the beams coming in directly from the window across from her.

The paper-thin walls allowed a pair of men's voices to travel through. The voices hadn't come from far.

Alyssa had no idea how long she'd been inside the closet. Her aching body said too long. She crawled out on all fours. A creek sounded. She froze, listening for the sounds of footsteps from down the hall.

When she was certain no one had heard, she sat down. She shook out her hands, trying to get some blood flowing.

The room had no dressers or chairs. There was a well-worn mattress pushed up to one corner of the room. It sat on the floor. No blanket. No pillow.

The trailer had the overall smell of a locker room if it sat dead center of a frat house. The greasy smell of day-old pizza and stale beer sent a wave of nausea slamming into her. Bile burned the back of her throat as she tried to swallow against a dry mouth.

The carpeting looked like a 1960's relic. Fear, sweat and desperation reeked. Looking around the room, her mind immediately snapped to a human trafficking ring. She sat back on her heels and held on to her belly. There was no way she was letting someone take her child.

"What does Bus Stop say the Judge wants?" A distinct male voice came through the wall. His voice was gruff and his words slow, like he had to think about each word.

"He wants answers. We can't hang on to her forever. She's too hot of a property. Anyone figures out she's missing, and the heat will come down." The second voice had more of a nasal-sounding pitch.

"I've done a lot of things with no problem, bro. You know me," Gruff said. "But torturing a pregnant lady seems all kinds of wrong. You know my baby is due next month. This one is about the same size as my girlfriend. I don't know about breaking someone's fingers in her condition."

"I hear you, bro. But how else you gonna get her to talk?" Nasal asked. "She's stubborn. You already saw that from earlier."

Alyssa performed a once-over on her body, checking her arms and legs for bruises. She found a massive one the size of a softball on her right hip.

"What if she don't give us what we want?" The fact Gruff didn't want to hurt her because he had a kid on the way sent an icy chill down her back. Was that the only reason she was still alive? That she hadn't been tortured? Maimed?

At least it didn't seem like they wanted to take her baby. The reality that she was the one they wanted didn't provide much relief. Hurt her and they were hurting her baby too.

"Then we have to suck it up and do our job, bro." Nasal was the more heartless of the two. Although, she doubted she'd see either one at Sunday church service anytime soon.

"I don't want to be the one to do it, bro." Gruff had a beating heart. She might be able to lean on his weakness. Find a way out of there safely.

The window that the sunlight had blasted through was too small to climb out of in her condition. The slats on the blinds looked like they'd gone through a tornado. With paper-thin walls, she couldn't risk making too much noise as she stood up and then crossed the room to get close to the door.

"Yeah? She's not worth my life. Push comes to shove, baby or not, I got no plans to die over a chick I don't even know." Nasal sounded determined.

The earth tilted on its axis as panic set in. The reality that those men were prepared to take her life slammed into her like a rogue wave on a sunny day. They obviously wanted something from her. What?

Alyssa should know what the two men were talking about but came up empty. Based on the conversation she'd overhead, there were others involved.

Nasal was clearly in charge and he thought she had something or knew something.

What?

She didn't even know who the Judge was let alone Bus Stop. Obviously, those were nicknames but not being able to remember was beyond frustrating. Searching her mind and drawing a hard blank was also scary.

How long had she been knocked out? A day? Two?

She had to be late term in her pregnancy based on her belly's size. Although, she couldn't exactly recall how far along she was. Her husband, Blake O'Connor, must be worried sick about her. *Blake*.

Hunger pangs picked that time to tell her that she must not have eaten in a while. She had no cell phone on her. No car keys in her pocket. No purse.

The only way to get out of the trailer she was in would be to walk right past Gruff and Nasal, and she highly doubted either would let her waltz out the door without a word. From the sounds of their conversation, their mentality was kill or be killed.

Or, maybe she could find a soft spot in the flooring and pick it open. The thought of sliding out underneath heaven knew what sent another ripple of fear through her. The ancient trailer seemed to be coming apart at the seams. Speaking of which, she moved to the mattress as quietly as she could and, with effort, shifted its position.

That's when she hit pay dirt. Whoever had been in the room before her had squirreled a hole in the corner. She peeled back rusted piece after rusted piece of rotting floor until she saw dirt. Her imagination picked that time to go wild. There had to be dozens of spiders and other insects down that hole. And what else? Rats? With only socks on her feet, she might be cut if there was any broken glass or jagged cans in there.

More possibilities crossed her mind and not ones she liked. The worst of her worries was the thought of insects crawling on her. She shivered at the thought. But she didn't see another choice.

Closing off her mind to all the potential creepy-crawlies that might be under there waiting for an opportunity like this one, she forced her thoughts to freedom instead. Getting out of there and away from those men was her only chance at keeping her baby alive. Alyssa had yet to officially meet the little bean growing in her belly, but she already knew she loved him or her.

The thought of seeing that little face in a few weeks or a month, based on her size, carried her through her fears as she slipped into the hole. She drew her right foot up almost immediately after touching down for fear that she'd stepped on a sharp object.

Rather than take the time to look around, she crawled on her hands and knees toward the lattice. At least there was enough light to see where to put her hands in front of her. The crawl space was about three feet deep.

A large something moved to her right. A rat? She swallowed a gasp and kept moving. Whatever was over there seemed to be trying to get away from her as much as she was trying to steer clear of it.

The first sound she heard when she emerged was the hum of vehicles on a highway. It was close. She had a shot at reaching it before they realized she was gone. The next thing she did was run her hand over her head and body, swiping at cobwebs.

Then, she grabbed hold of her belly and made a run for it.

THE SUN WAS coming up, signaling the end of another deep night shift for Blake O'Connor. These shifts were killing him. He hadn't worked the overnight shift in years when he'd volunteered for the grind after being served divorce papers six months ago.

The idea of sleeping alone every night had been too much and, besides, it wasn't like he got any sleep after Alyssa left him anyway. His Houston apartment had never felt emptier than when she'd cleared out her belongings. Hell, she hadn't even left her citrus-smelling shampoo behind. And he hadn't been able to eat an orange or grapefruit since. Even lemons reminded him of her.

The separation that was supposed to give his new wife time to figure out what she really wanted after her father's death had turned into divorce. No explanation. No discussion. No chance to make it right.

Just the term *irreconcilable differences* listed as the reason.

What did that even mean?

Yeah, he was still chewing on that bitter pill all these months later. So much for being able to let it go and move on with his life.

Being on the force and having a routine—which he'd been ready to quit so the two of them could move back to the O'Connor family ranch in Katy Gulch and claim his birth rite—was keeping him sane.

Blake came from a tight-knit ranching family, one of the most successful in Texas. The O'Connors were a close bunch. He figured part of the reason they were taught to love one another was because his parents had survived their worst nightmare. Their six-month-old daughter, and Blake's only sister, had been a kidnapping target decades ago. Despite years of searching, neither the infant nor her abductors were ever found. His mother might have been forced to move on from the tragedy, but she never stopped thinking about Caroline or hoping for her child's safe return.

A few weeks after the kidnapping, his mother leaned she was pregnant again. She credited the pregnancy as being her saving grace. For the sake of her growing family, she'd forced herself to pick up the pieces of her life and carry on when she'd been so devastated that she'd wanted to stop living.

The kidnapper's trail might have dried up decades

ago, but new evidence had come to light that had Blake and his brothers revisiting the cold case. Their father had been killed after taking it upon himself to investigate and life generally had been turned up-side-down.

So, yeah, tired didn't begin to cover just how much he needed to face-plant in his bed right now.

Blake pulled into his complex and navigated around to the back of his townhouse. He had an end unit, which let in a little more sunlight. He'd more or less adapted to city life after growing up on a ranch with acreage to spare.

On his twenty-first birthday, like each of his siblings, he'd been handed keys to his own home on the property. That's where he went to spend his days off and every vacation. He came home as often as he could during calving season to help out.

Pulling into the garage, the hairs on Blake's neck pricked. The feeling that something was off settled over him.

The trash can, he realized, had been pushed up against the wall. It wasn't trash day and he knew for a fact he hadn't been the one to move it.

He parked and kept the garage door open. With an eye on his side-view mirror, he caught someone trying to slip inside.

Was this person kidding him? Hand on his gun, he removed the safety strap. He kept low as he opened the door. Climbing out, he moved so that the tire would cover him.

"Hands where I can see them." His demand came as he moved around to the back of his vehicle.

Weapon leading the way, he used the Jeep as cover. When no response came, he repeated the command.

"I'm alone. Don't shoot." The familiar female voice caused his heart to freefall.

At first, he didn't believe Alyssa could be standing inside his garage. A glance in her direction confirmed her presence. It was definitely her. But what he saw nearly cut a hole in the center of his chest.

She was pregnant.

Chapter Two

"Close the garage door, please." Alyssa glanced around like she expected someone to jump out from behind a box. The desperation in her voice tried to put a chink in his armor. *Not happening.*

The fact Blake had fallen for her once and had the scars to prove it was enough of a deterrent to keep him from going down that road again.

"Give me one reason to listen to you," he said. Yeah, he was being stubborn, but he didn't exactly have a reason to trust her. Her blue eyes were huge. Her chestnut hair was shoulder-length now and just as beautiful.

At five feet five inches, she came in at average height, but that's where *typical* ended for Alyssa. She'd been the real deal; intelligence, sense of humor and the kind of inside-out beauty that had left him speechless. And still did if he was being completely honest.

"What's wrong, Blake?" She cradled her bump and stared at him like she was shocked at his reaction.

"What did you expect, Alyssa? A welcome-home speech? A hug? You walked out on me without a word—"

"What are you talking about?" Confusion knitted her brows together. She quickly recovered, looking around like she was in a horror movie.

He walked over and tapped the garage door button so it would close. She could walk out the front door this time if she wanted to leave him.

Without another word, and mainly because he needed a second to pull himself together, he turned and walked inside the townhouse. He left the door open, figuring she could do what she wanted.

Since sleep didn't seem like it was happening anytime soon, Blake walked over to the fridge and grabbed a cold brew coffee. Normally he'd put on a pot, but he didn't expect her to stick around.

By the time he unscrewed the lid and turned around, she'd stepped into the hallway and closed the door behind her.

"You don't seem happy to see me. Or worried." The shock and disappointment in her voice caught him off guard. "They said if word got out about me there'd be trouble." She stared at him blankly. She practically mumbled and he had to strain to hear her. "No, they used the word *heat*. There'd be heat."

Blake forced his feelings of frustration and anger aside. He took a good look at the pregnant woman standing in his hallway. She wasn't wearing shoes. She stood there in her socks. She had on a maternity

T-shirt and jeans. Her belly looked like she was ready to pop. And she was dirty, head to toe.

He also realized she smelled like…

Out of consideration for her feelings and respect for their past, he decided not to name the scent. It was a far cry from the citrusy clean he was used to and missed.

"It looks like you're in some kind of trouble." His words came out a little harsher than he wanted. He took a sip of coffee and a deep breath. "Let's start over. Why are you here?"

"Because you're my husband and I thought you'd be worried about me." She looked at him like he had two heads.

"*Was* your husband. You divorced me," he corrected.

"Why would I do that?"

"You tell me and we'll both know," he fired back a little too quickly. Blake raked a hand through his hair before taking another sip. "Obviously, you're in some kind of trouble. Can I call someone?"

She shook her head. "There is no one, Blake."

At least she got his name right.

A fleeting thought she might be playing a twisted joke on him shot another round of anger through him. He reminded himself no one he'd cared about could be that cruel.

"You're pregnant. Is that why you left me? Was it for the baby's father?" He couldn't help but ask. This situation pretty much ranked right up there with the most bizarre of his life, and the pain nearly gutted him.

"If that was the reason, I'd still be here. It's *your* baby, Blake." More of that hurt and confusion laced her tone.

There had to be a logical explanation for his ex-wife showing up at his home, pregnant, after walking out and filing divorce papers months ago. Did the real father walk out and now she was trying to circle back and take some of the O'Connor family fortune? Blake dismissed the thought. She hadn't asked for one red cent in the divorce, which had been finalized. The Alyssa he knew would be too proud to come begging for money even if she was desperate. She was resourceful and would find a way. Losing her dad had taken a toll on her and their marriage.

Since she wasn't the type of person to rub his nose in the fact that their relationship had failed, he had no idea what she was really doing on his doorstep. He couldn't help but think that *he'd* failed in some way and yet he'd racked his brain trying to solve that puzzle for weeks after she'd bolted.

"You said you needed time, Alyssa. I gave it to you." And those were the last words said between husband and wife before she took off and he'd been served papers.

It took a few seconds to register that she'd said *he* was the father. He didn't know a whole lot about pregnancies and yet he wondered if it was possible.

"How far along are you?" he asked, knowing she

could very well lie. It wasn't her style. She'd rather walk away like she had before.

"Eight months? Nine? I have to be getting close… right?" She cradled her bump, cocked her head to one side, and then studied him. She'd served him divorce papers six months ago after walking out almost two months prior to that. And, yeah, they'd had a physical relationship. A damn good one. The timing couldn't be ignored, and a quick test could prove paternity.

"I'm sorry. Maybe I shouldn't have come here." Alyssa brought her hand up to her head, rubbing her temple.

The hell she was getting away from him after dropping that bomb.

"Start at the beginning and tell me everything that happened to lead you to my doorstep today." He motioned toward a pair of chairs tucked underneath a lip of the granite island. She'd insisted on a white kitchen when they'd picked out the place.

She'd fallen in love with the townhouse after they'd married. The open floorplan and white kitchen with stainless steel appliances had sold her before she made it upstairs to see a pair of bedrooms and an office.

"I don't remember a whole lot, actually." She shook her head and stayed firmly positioned next to the garage door, looking like she might bolt if someone said "Boo."

Switching to cop mode, he acknowledged that he needed to distance himself from his personal feelings if he wanted answers. Softening his stance and his tone, he asked, "Would you like a glass of water?"

She nodded and pressed her lips into a thin line. With her arms cradling her bump and a determined set to her chin, he'd put her on the defensive.

His bad. He retrieved a glass of water and filled it from the tap. Instead of walking it over to her, he set it down on the granite island in front of a bar chair. "Okay to put it here?"

This time, she nodded before walking over and taking a seat. She took a sip of water and then held on to the glass, rolling it around in her hands.

Keeping her gaze trained on the lines in the white granite, she said, "I'm sorry."

"For what?" he shot back a little too quickly. Maintaining the facade that he wasn't affected by her sitting in his kitchen again wasn't going so well.

"Whatever it was I did that put that scowl on your face when you look at me."

Damned if those words didn't score a direct hit and shatter some of his resolve.

ALYSSA WISHED LIKE anything that she could remember what had happened. She'd tried to cover up just how devastated she was by Blake's rejection but that was impossible.

Everything in her heart said they were still in love. Showing up here, hiding until he came home, had led to the second biggest shock of her day—learning they were divorced.

Blake looked at her like he didn't believe the baby was his. She might not remember a whole lot right now, but she knew in her bones this baby belonged to Blake.

And yet she couldn't ignore the shocked look on his face when he'd found out she was pregnant. The surprises were adding up today. None of them were good.

Looking at him with his six feet three inches of solid muscle and dark roast eyes, her heart free-fell. It suddenly occurred to her that as good as he looked with his made-from-granite jawline and high cheekbones, she was quite the opposite. All grunge and dirt.

To top it off, she smelled so bad that she could smell herself. *Ripe* didn't begin to cover it and her clothes were literally crunchy.

Running toward the man she loved—and she knew without a doubt that she loved Blake—wasn't supposed to end with him being shocked about the pregnancy and her learning they were divorced. Confusion settled in as the place that was supposed to be her safe haven had just become hell. And all she could say was, "I should go."

"Where?" His stone face was unreadable now.

"I'm not sure. Anywhere would be better than here." She hadn't meant to say those words out loud despite the fact they were true.

He drew back like she'd slapped him in the face.

A few seconds later, he released the breath he'd been holding, slowly, like he was twisting a release valve.

"How did you get here?" He started asking practical questions and she could tell he had gone into cop mode. It was probably a good idea to put some emotional distance between them, except that every muscle inside her body wanted to reach out to him, touch him, feel the comfort she'd always felt when she was close to him—comfort that was burned into her muscle memory.

She took another sip of water. "I hitchhiked."

The sharp intake of air caused her to look up at him.

"Before you tell me how dangerous that was, I barely escaped a trailer with two men having a conversation about who was going to torture me to get me to talk. Hitchhiking was the least of my problems," she noted.

The look of shock on his face was followed by him studying her intently. "Fair point. Any idea where this trailer park is located?"

"I had the driver pull off at a gas station nearby where I requested a clerk call the police and send them to a blue-and-white trailer in Bendy Park off the highway. It was the only one I saw with a red awning, but I didn't exactly stick around once I broke up enough of the floor to climb out. There was about a four-foot clearance underneath and a white lattice that I managed to move enough to slip out." It all sounded so surreal when she heard herself talk about it. Like it was some crazy dream that she'd wake up from any minute.

Blake scanned her and she figured he was looking for injuries or a sign of sexual assault.

"I have a bruise the size of Phoenix on my right hip but came to in the trailer with my clothes on. All except for my favorite pair of boots that I'm certain I had on," she explained, her pulse racing as the nightmare-worthy memory resurfaced.

"What about other injuries?" he asked.

Oh, right. "My head. I felt around and found a pump knot along with some dried blood."

"A hit to the head could explain your confusion and memory loss." He'd moved to his laptop and opened it. "I'm guessing you haven't seen a doctor."

"They're planning to hurt me or worse and I immediately came here." She cradled her bump. "I thought they might have someone waiting at a hospital and decided not to go anywhere they could easily find me."

Blake stood there and stared at her like he was looking right through her. He could practically read her mind in the past and they'd joked about having a mental connection that made words unnecessary at times, but that was before. Her brains were so scrambled now she couldn't even remember what had happened to their marriage—a marriage that was one of the first things she'd thought about when she'd opened her eyes and realized she was in trouble.

He motioned toward her stomach. "I'm guessing

that's the reason. There are half a dozen baby rings operating in south Texas." His gaze faltered when he asked, "Boy or girl?"

"Does it matter?" she asked. The baby-ring idea didn't mesh with what she'd overheard. "They said something about getting information from me."

"Okay, I can take your statement here. And I can bring a doctor to the house," he started, and she noticed he didn't answer her question.

She put a hand up to stop him.

"The men in the trailer said there'd be a lot of heat if people realized I was missing. I thought they meant because of you. But if we're divorced, why would you care?" She couldn't figure that one out.

"I'm sure they have their reasons," he stated and the coldness in his voice shot right through her.

"Don't worry, I won't be a burden to you. I'll find a place to stay." She didn't bother to hide her defensiveness.

"It's not safe for you to leave if you don't have somewhere to go and, besides, you're a witness. I need you here to collect more information so these jerks can be tracked down and stopped." He was being reasonable whereas she was wrung out from emotion and his rejection.

"I'll find another place to stay after I give you my statement." She didn't say, *where I'm wanted*, even though the words came to mind.

"Alyssa, I'd like you to stay here until we can figure out what's going on." Those words, spoken with compassion instead of judgment, made her rethink the snappy response on her tongue trying to escape.

"Okay." She had no idea where that word came from when all her warning sirens were going off inside her head with the shock of a spring tornado on an otherwise sunny day. Staying with him made sense, but could she?

Chapter Three

"I guess not." If the baby was Blake's it would have the same rights as every O'Connor. The sex of the child made no difference. It was curiosity he couldn't afford to let take hold until he had confirmation the child was his.

Did he doubt Alyssa's word?

Considering the fact she couldn't remember where she was yesterday or how she'd ended up in a trailer alone with two men intent on hurting her, Blake had reservations about her having some type of brain trauma. If she was in her right mind would he doubt the baby was his? The timeline fit and, despite his hurt, he didn't think she would lie about something this important. But where had she been and why had she been keeping the pregnancy from him? First things first, he needed to get her out of present danger and lock away the bastards who'd been at the trailer.

"I'm off duty but I can make a call to see what happened at the trailer after you left." He looked at her, trying to ignore how much his pulse raced while she was in the same room and how much he wanted to haul her into his arms and make reassurances he couldn't guarantee.

She nodded. "I'd appreciate it."

The bastards might already be in jail. Problem solved.

Blake fished out his cell. He planned to call his friend and former partner, Liz Roark. Since he'd switched to the night shift, he'd been stuck with a rookie ever since. The area of town Alyssa had described was Liz's beat. It was possible she'd taken the call from Dispatch, but that was probably hoping too much.

He hit her name in his contacts and put the call on speaker. She answered on the first ring.

"Aren't you supposed to be home with your face stuffed in a pillow by now, O'Connor?" Liz asked.

Alyssa bristled at the closeness between him and Liz. She'd never said anything directly, but he'd had the sense she didn't like their relationship. Blake didn't figure this was the time to remind Alyssa that she'd been the one to walk out and shut the door on their relationship or that he'd never once flirted or cheated.

Cops were extended family and had each other's backs in life-and-death situations. The job required a closeness unlike most professions.

"Sleep had to wait. I have Alyssa here and you're

on speaker." It was that moment he realized he should've prepared Liz better.

"Oh." There was a whole conversation in that one little word and a whole lot of disapproval. Then a whole lot of silence.

"There was a call." He looked to Alyssa for a timeframe. She held up a lone finger. "About an hour ago. It would've come from a convenience store clerk asking for a check on a trailer in Bendy Park off the highway."

"Ah, right. Farley took that one. Why?"

"What can you tell me about it?" he asked.

"Not much. There was no answer when Farley knocked on the door. No vehicles in front of the blue-and-white building. Then, when Farley was pulling away, he saw two guys exit the trailer and take off running. They were average height and weight, both Caucasian males described as having dark hair and wearing jeans and hoodies. They must have had a vehicle stashed nearby because Farley gave chase, but they disappeared like ghosts," she informed.

"And the trailer? What condition was it in?" he asked.

"Honestly? The place looked like it was used for trafficking. The back bedroom had an old mattress, and someone pulled up the flooring in order to climb out. Pretty smart actually but I can't imagine going underneath with all those spiders." She made a shudder-like noise.

Blake confirmed Alyssa's story as she sat there.

Her chin jutted out as she listened, like hearing the details again wouldn't break her in the least. Strength was another one of those amazing traits of hers that he didn't want to think too much about.

"Any idea who these perps were?" he asked.

"Not in the least. Farley has been trying to track down the manager of the park to see who owns or rents the trailer. My guess is that he won't get far."

Alyssa's shoulders deflated. She had to be uncomfortable in those dirty clothes and the fact she hadn't been able to take a shower in—who knew how long?—must have her wanting to scrub herself down with just about anything she could get her hands on.

He couldn't count the number of times she'd threatened to hose him down before letting him come inside the house at the ranch after a long day working cattle. The memory almost had him smiling.

Blake shifted his gaze to Alyssa and waited for her to make the call on revealing herself.

She gave a curt nod.

"The victim who climbed out the bedroom flooring happens to be sitting in my kitchen right now and she's the one on speaker," he told Liz.

"I'm thirty minutes away. I'll be right over." She didn't give him time to argue before she ended the call.

Alyssa issued a sharp breath.

"You're welcome to use the shower if you'd like to clean up," he offered. "You have plenty of time before she gets here."

She sat there for a long moment, looking like she didn't know where to start.

"That would be amazing actually," she finally said. Her response shouldn't have made his chest fill with pride. He tried to blame his weakness on her condition. He wanted to make the mother of his child—if that was the situation—comfortable. He also wanted to get more details about the case and assess the danger she was in. "But...what would I wear?"

"I can take your clothes and throw them in the wash if—"

"I'd rather burn them." The way she said the words made him realize she would remember waking up in that trailer in conditions that didn't sound humane if she put those clothes back on.

"There's a jogging outfit of yours and a few other things folded in the master bathroom. You must've forgotten to pack the hair dryer." Mentioning the manner in which she'd left things had him hearing the frustration in his own voice.

"Okay." Based on her response, she'd picked up on it too.

"Are you hungry?" he asked.

"Starving." She patted her pockets. "But I don't have any way to repay you."

He was already shaking his head before she finished her sentence. It was the least he could do for someone in need. "It's nothing. I'll order pizza. It'll be here by the time you finish showering."

"Sounds good. Thank you."

He nodded and waved her off. Blake had ranching in his blood and ranchers always helped each other out. No amount of bad blood would cause him to turn away his pregnant ex after she'd been abducted.

"You still like pepperoni and mushroom?" he asked.

A small smile upturned the corners of her lips. It didn't reach her eyes. "Yes."

He turned away because looking at her wasn't doing great things to his resolve. His bruised ego wanted to demand answers about why she'd walked out, but reason said this wasn't the time to press for those answers.

Once this was over, he intended to sit her down and get the answers he'd been searching for. A frustrating voice in the back of his mind asked what good that would do. She'd still be pregnant with his child. The evidence, the timeline, pointed toward the child being his. Maybe it was time to move forward and think about how they planned to bring up this kid.

So, why couldn't his heart get the message? Because it wanted more than weekends and every other Christmas with a family.

ALYSSA PEELED OFF the filthy clothes and placed them in the trash bag she'd retrieved from underneath the sink before heading to the bathroom. She placed each piece in a plastic bag, never wanting to see them again, but realizing law enforcement would most likely want them as evidence, before retrieving the clothes Blake mentioned from the closet.

Being back in the townhouse she'd shared with him felt like the most normal thing despite the crazy and heavy circumstances that brought her here. His reaction was the only out-of-place thing. There was no way he would have turned her down, not when she'd shown up in this condition, pregnant and looking every bit like the experience she'd just had. But it was clear he was doing this only because she was pregnant and desperate. She could see the hurt in his eyes, hurt that she'd caused, and it had nearly wrung her out. Not being able to remember anything before the trailer except her marriage to Blake and where they'd lived was like living in a nightmare. Questions were mounting, but thinking too hard gave her a headache. She reached up and ran her fingers across the lump on the back of her skull. The spot was tender, and she immediately withdrew her hand.

She remembered the male voices in the other room at the trailer. But she couldn't remember exactly what they'd said. Something niggled at the back of her mind and was just out of reach.

After tossing the last of her clothes into the bag, she pulled the drawstrings tightly to close it. She set the bag in the hallway and then closed the bathroom door, wanting to get as far away from the stench as possible.

Footsteps coming down the hallway had her stepping away from the door as quickly as she could.

Being naked and near Blake used to feel so normal. Now she would cover up even through a closed door except that she didn't want to get that smell on a towel or bathrobe.

"I'll hold on to these for Liz." Blake's deep timbre still had the ability to send warmth spiraling through her. Being near him had a way of heightening all her senses and stirring up emotions best left alone under the circumstances.

"Thank you." She couldn't imagine any reason that would have caused her to walk away from Blake O'Connor, except that she'd done just that. The evidence was indisputable. Her heart ached being so close to him as anger came off him in palpable waves.

Could she blame him?

No. She couldn't. If the tables were turned, she would feel the same way. Blake's honor code would stop him from turning her away despite being done with the marriage—again, totally on her, apparently.

She just wished she knew what could have caused her to leave him in the first place. Because she might not have all her memories back, but being near him brought an onslaught of emotion—happy emotion. And she'd been one hundred percent certain they'd had a happy marriage.

Alyssa's brain cramped, so she stopped that train of thought. It was unproductive anyway. She could probably fill a library with things she couldn't remember and trying to force it seemed to make it only worse.

Stepping into the warm water and with memories all around her, she let herself get lost in the feeling of familiarity. She could wrestle with her mind later.

After scrubbing for a solid twenty minutes, she finally cut off the water. Stepping out of the shower and maneuvering around with her bump proved interesting. She'd forgotten how little things like drying her own feet were more complicated now.

She dropped a towel on the floor and stepped on it. Problem solved. If only all of life's problems could be handled so easily. Taking a sidestep, she managed to scoop up the towel. She hung it over the shower door to dry.

Her clothes were folded and stacked on top of the counter. There was no way she was fitting into her old bra, but the oversize shirt should cover her. Her jogging pants wouldn't go over her big belly, but she could tuck them down underneath and make do.

It felt so good to be clean again.

Hunger pangs reminded her it was past time to eat. She couldn't remember her last meal. Her head still ached, and she didn't figure it would be safe to take anything for it.

She missed coffee and an occasional glass of wine. But every time she thought about meeting her baby, the sacrifices seemed worth it. The baby started moving around, kicking and stretching.

After brushing her hair and teeth, using spares

that were kept in the drawer, she hurried to Blake in the kitchen. Officer Liz wasn't there yet.

Alyssa practically beamed at Blake who was plating a couple pieces of her favorite pizza.

"You have to feel this," she said to him before she really thought it through.

His muscles tensed as he set down a plate. His gaze never moved from her face. His intention clear—he wasn't ready to deal with the baby.

Hope she never should have allowed in the first place deflated her chest.

"I'm sorry, Alyssa. I just can't right now." His words were daggers to the chest.

Chapter Four

"You should eat." Blake pointed to her plate. He'd set out napkins and a glass of water for her.

He flexed and released his fingers a couple of times in an attempt to work off some of his tension. Tension at seeing his ex looking vulnerable and alone. Tension at the thought he might become a father in a matter of days or weeks in what was the shock of all shocks to his system. Could he even get used to the idea? The possibility?

Her smile didn't have the same spark as when he found her outside. She'd looked so certain he would be happy to see her and a piece of him—a piece he didn't want to acknowledge or feed—had hated letting her down. Blake chalked it up to being a nice person.

"Mind if I sit at the table?" she asked.

"Be my guest." The words might be natural in a situation like this, but they sounded all wrong saying them to her.

Another awkward moment passed between them.

Another smile that died on her lips when she made eye contact.

What could he say? This wasn't easy. A knock sounded at the door, no doubt signaling Liz's arrival. Blake was already standing at the kitchen pass-through, so he walked to the back door of the townhouse. Liz always knew to park in front of his garage.

He opened the door. "Welcome to my circus."

Liz was five feet two of black-haired dynamite. "How are you?" She studied him.

"Fine." Officers were so good at putting up a facade that he was certain she was convinced.

Until she took a step inside and brought him into a hug. "No. Really. How are you?"

The move shocked him, but she was genuinely a friend and showing support. There wasn't anything sexual about their contact. It was buddy to buddy. The equivalent of a bear hug and pat on the shoulder after a pickup game of basketball.

"Honestly? I'm shocked. Check it out for yourself." He put his arm out, hand extended, like he was presenting the hallway in the way someone unveils a new car.

Liz gave him a look of solidarity, which he appreciated, and then stalked into the kitchen. "Hey, Alyssa. Long time no see."

The look of shock on Alyssa's face at the off-handed comment rattled Blake. It must have had the same effect on Liz because she immediately put her hands up in the surrender position with her palms out.

"I didn't mean it like—"

"No. It's fine." The defensiveness in Alyssa's voice meant she was anything but. The forced smile didn't help matters.

"It was a jerk thing to say. I didn't mean it like—"

"Already forgotten." Alyssa pushed to standing and walked over to Liz. She stuck her hand out between them. "Good to see you again, Liz."

Liz took the offering. "You too."

When it seemed polite to step away, Alyssa returned to her plate. "I don't know the last time I had a decent meal, so do you mind if I continue eating?"

"No. Of course not. Go ahead." Liz followed her and took a seat on the opposite side of the table. "Smells great."

"There's plenty here if you want a slice."

"No. Thanks. I was just commenting on the smell," she said.

Well, if this conversation wasn't awkward, Blake didn't know what was.

"Blake tells me that you had an incident with a trailer park. Can you tell me what happened in your own words?" Liz's demeanor changed to all business. She sat up a little straighter as she took out a notebook and pen.

Reports were filed online now but some cops preferred to jot down a few notes the old-fashioned way first. Then the report could be filed once details were gathered.

He listened as Alyssa recounted her story in between bites. It was almost word-for-word what she'd told him.

A stunned Liz jotted a few notes. She nodded her head and repeated a few uh-huhs. "Do you have a physical description of either of the men?"

"Afraid not. When I came to, they were in the next room. I didn't think it was a good idea to traipse through the living room or alert them to the fact I was awake. Once I got out of there, I didn't look back." There was terror in her voice and Blake had to fight the urge to sit down beside her or take her hand in his like he'd done so many times in the past to comfort her. They didn't belong to each other anymore and it wasn't his place. Besides, with her carrying his child—possibly—he would need to remain impartial. He couldn't fathom having a family under these circumstances.

"You said you overhead the pair of men, is that correct?" Liz's voice had a sharp edge to it. He chalked it up to her being protective of him.

"Yes."

"Do you think you could recognize their voices again if you heard them?" Liz studied Alyssa. Was she assessing her to see if she could be trusted?

"I'm not sure. It all happened so fast and I couldn't get away from there fast enough." She brought her hand up to rub her temple, a move that said her stress levels were shooting up. Talking about the incident made her relive it. He told himself it only bothered him because stress wasn't good for her child. On that note, Liz's judgmental voice wasn't helping.

"Can you come back in a few hours, Liz?"

"Yes. Sure. I guess so." His former partner looked more than a little dumbfounded at the suggestion.

He could sense Alyssa's tension rising with Liz in the room. It had been a mistake to allow her to come here. They could finish the interview over the phone, or he could take down the details and shoot an email. He grabbed the bag of clothes that his ex had brought down from the bathroom, and then handed them over as evidence. "This is what she was wearing. Would you mind having them checked for any possible DNA evidence?"

"Yeah." She shrugged like it was no big deal, and then took the bag. "Of course, I can."

"Thank you. If you don't mind starting there. Alyssa has already given her statement. These are the clothes she wore. If you have any questions, you know my number." He started walking her out, needing to get Alyssa's stress levels down immediately. He didn't have a ton of experience with pregnant women, not personally, but he didn't want her going into early labor.

"Fine." Liz caught his gaze. "Walk me out?"

Blake nodded before turning to Alyssa. "I'll just be a minute."

Lips pursed together like it was taking all her energy to hold her tongue, she seemed to give up when she half smiled. "Take your time. I'm not going anywhere."

"Good to see you again, Alyssa." Liz's tone wasn't helping, especially considering how forced the statement sounded.

He would deal with the fallout in a few minutes. Suddenly, a quick walk outside seemed like a good idea. Grab some fresh air, and maybe find some perspective. Because his protective instincts flared no matter how many times he reminded himself how burned he'd been after Alyssa walked out.

Liz led the way and he followed. He barely had the door closed when she whirled around on him and pointed her finger in his chest. "Are you kidding me right now?"

"What's that supposed to mean?"

"We've been working together a long time. Your ex-wife is pregnant and shows up at your house, so you just let her in? And what? The past eight months of you being miserable are suddenly erased? The divorce she asked for doesn't exist? The way she treated you doesn't matter anymore?"

"I'm better now." He was being honest. Technically, he was better. Was he completely over the pain? No. But that didn't mean he wasn't better.

"Yeah? Since when? A couple of weeks ago? You finally move on and she's back to mess with your head?" There was fire in Liz's eyes. More of that fire came out when she spoke. She stood there, arms folded over her chest like a schoolteacher scolding the class for talking too much. Heat poured off her in palpable waves.

"It's not like that." He shouldn't want to defend Alyssa, but he'd loved her enough to believe they had a future together, to marry her, and he couldn't have anyone else insulting her. Plus, Liz's reaction was full tilt.

"Then, how? Educate me. Because all I'm seeing right now is more heartache and the first round nearly broke you. So what happens next?"

He shifted his weight and turned to look away. Denying he'd taken the divorce hard wouldn't do any good. Liz had been an eyewitness to his pain. Front row. So, he would cut her some slack.

After a couple of breaths, he continued, "I hear you. Hell, I appreciate you for wanting to step in and make sure I'm not going down a road we both know won't be good for me."

"It's what partners do for each other. Even former ones." She shrugged a shoulder like it was no big deal. "Plus, we're friends."

"Trust me when I say that I'm good, Liz."

She shot him the look. The one that said just how much she didn't believe him right then.

"Fair enough," he conceded. His judgment had obviously been off when he married Alyssa. And the pregnancy complicated matters. "How about this. I'll take it easy. I'll make sure that I don't fall into that same old trap as before, thinking that she loved me when she couldn't have, or she wouldn't have been able to walk out so easily."

"That's better." Liz's stance had softened somewhat. Her shoulder muscles relaxed, and she seemed to finally exhale. Then, she locked on to his gaze. "Is the baby yours?"

"The question is out of bounds and you know it." The truth was that her guess was as good as his on that one. Even so, he didn't want to go there with her.

"Fine. Just don't come to me when she breaks your heart again." She started to take off in a huff.

"Point taken." It was his turn to stand there, arms folded across his chest. Being a friend was one thing. Telling someone how to run their life was another. He didn't like the turn the conversation had taken.

Rather than poke the bear, he watched as she got into her vehicle, and then drove off. It was good to know where they stood.

THIS WAS THE first time Alyssa didn't want to be a fly on the wall, listening in on a conversation she knew very well was about her. Liz used to be Blake's partner. The two were obviously still close. The woman couldn't possibly have anything good to say about Alyssa.

The sheer look of shock on Liz's face when her gaze had dropped down to Alyssa's stomach said it all. Liz was probably outside trying to convince Blake to run far away or kick Alyssa out. So, she sat there and finished up her pizza, trying to remember anything she could about the past few days because dwelling on something she couldn't change wouldn't be her smartest move.

There was a notepad and pen on the dining table. Alyssa grabbed them both and wrote down everything she knew. The blue-and-white trailer she'd been in with the red awning. The sign, Bendy Park, she'd run past on her way to the highway.

The voices. One she remembered as Nasal. She wrote *heartless* next to his name. Gruff had a softer side. And then it came to her. Gruff had said his girlfriend was pregnant and due soon. She suddenly remembered he hadn't wanted to break her finger.

Nasal and Gruff needed information from her. They wanted her to talk. How could she remember anything after they knocked her on the head?

How many people were involved? She wrote the question down. Nasal and Gruff might have been glorified babysitters, or, like they'd openly discussed, in charge of getting information out of her. The images of the two of them in her head meant Nasal was tall and thin with a big nose. Gruff, on the other hand, she pictured as someone who was short and thick with dark hair and eyes. He had an accent when he spoke…northeast?

Heads were going to roll because of her escape. There was an urgency to both of their tones when they discussed the need to get information from her. Did they report to Bus Stop and the Judge?

Alyssa cradled her bump, grateful the little bean seemed to be okay despite being extra quiet.

The back door opened and closed. Alyssa instinctively tore off the sheet of paper and folded it. She picked up her plate and held the notes against the bottom and out of view.

Walking toward the kitchen, she had to pass Blake in the short hallway.

"Excuse me," she said, trying to slide past by turning to the side. Didn't help, considering her bump was large and she ended up grazing his arm. "Sorry."

"No. You're good. Can I take that?" He motioned toward the plate. She'd never seen an arm move so fast as when his had accidentally touched her.

"I got it," she said quickly, a little too quickly. She shot him a look of apology. "I'm good. I remember where everything goes, and I figure it's good for me to stand up. I was in a cramped space for God knows how long and pretty much every bone in my body aches right now. All my joints are stiff. I need blood circulation."

He nodded. His reaction was short of sympathetic. "Liz can put together a timeline and we can probably figure out how many hours or days you were missing. We can pull your phone records and see when the last time you texted someone was or the last time your phone was used and that might give us a ballpark."

"Good idea." Of course, he was a cop. Naturally, he would think of all the things she didn't. He was good at his job too.

"I remember sort of coming in and out of consciousness. I have images of being awake and hearing voices, but it's impossible to separate fact from fiction if that makes any sense."

"It'll come back to you." He said the words too causally to mean them. If there'd been walls up between them before, there were entire buildings now. "Instead of bringing in a doctor, which could take more time, maybe you and I should head to the ER."

"No." She shook her head for emphasis. "Absolutely not." Panic was rising inside her, causing her pulse to race and heat to climb up her neck.

"We don't have to leave right now." He studied her and she could tell he was assessing her mental state by the way his gaze narrowed as it traveled over her.

"I'm good. Of course, I'm shaken up. Who wouldn't be after coming to in a trailer with strangers in the next room and a lump on their head?" She made a show of looking at her arms, body and legs. "Physically, I'm fine other than a few bumps and bruises. I'm not cramping or bleeding."

The little bean picked that moment to kick Alyssa's ribs from the inside out. She sucked in a breath, holding her stomach with her free hand until the pain subsided. Next came a mind-numbing cramp.

"Alyssa? What just happened?"

"Not labor if that's what you're worried about." She took in a couple more breaths, trying to ride out the waves of pain. She told herself this was normal.

She'd had a few of these recently and remembered asking her doctor about them.

"I wouldn't know the first thing about pregnancy or labor, but it's clear that you need to be checked out by a doctor—"

She started to mount an argument, but he put up a hand to stop her.

"Hear me out." He waited for an answer.

She nodded, figuring it couldn't hurt. Besides, he was going out of his way to help her when most would have turned her away. Crazy that the last thing she remembered was being married to him. And smiling. She remembered being happy too.

"I'll have someone come here. I have a good relationship with a few ER docs. I'll just see if anyone can come here to give you an exam."

She blinked at him for a long moment. He was serious. And then it dawned on her that he came from one of the wealthiest cattle ranching families in Texas. Despite his humble lifestyle and the fact he had a normal job, he had more zeroes in his bank account than she would ever see in a lifetime. He could easily pay someone for a house call. But it was dangerous to bring anyone else here.

"What if those men know where you live? What if staying here is a bad idea?" Panic seized her chest as another cramp caused her to plant her hand against the wall. "I can't go back in that small closet again."

"Alyssa."

"I'm okay. It's good. Don't worry." The pain was

bad but it had been worse. "Go ahead. What were you saying before?"

"First and foremost, I'm a cop. They'd have to be pretty stupid to show up at my home. Plus, Liz stops by sometimes. She was just here. I have people coming in and out. There's nothing unusual going on if people visit me." The reality that his former partner visited his home on a frequent basis shouldn't send a stab of jealousy ripping through her even though it did.

Agreeing to let a doctor examine her was probably a good idea when she really thought about it. Alyssa wasn't worried so much about herself, but when it came to the little bean, she would do anything to make sure the pregnancy was on track. If that meant subjecting herself to an exam by a stranger, so be it.

"You can arrange for a doctor to come here?" Blake was an O'Connor. He could afford pretty much anything he wanted. It was easy to forget considering that he worked in law enforcement like several of his brothers, despite having been born into one of the wealthiest cattle ranching families in Texas.

He shot her an embarrassed look. The man was one of the most down-to-earth people she'd ever met. In fact, he drove an inexpensive Jeep and wore jeans and boots most of the time. He had the kind of good looks that could sell a million albums on the country and western charts. Take his cowboy hat off and he could be on a mainstream billboard.

"Okay if I put this away?" She motioned toward the kitchen.

"You're my guest. I don't mind cleaning up." He held his hand out. The words rolled off his tongue so easily. He was used to living here without her, which meant she'd left a long time ago.

She drew in a sharp breath. He was right. She no longer lived here. And yet it still knocked the breath out of her to hear him say it so easily.

Chapter Five

"What is that?" Blake saw something in Alyssa's hand after she passed the plate over to him.

"My back hurts. Okay if I sit down?" She turned away from him and started walking toward the living room. Did she think he would let her get away without answering his question so easily? Blake set the plate on the counter and then followed her. If he was going to help her, he needed the facts. He needed honesty from her.

"You can do anything you want." He heard the way that sounded and decided to take another tack. "Do what you need to, but answer my question."

"While you were outside, I tried my best to remember anything and everything from the trailer. It feels like the sky is going to fall on top of you if I share any information." She'd crumbled the page in her hand. It was now the size of a golf ball.

Blake needed to get the doctor en route, so he fired off a text, asking Liz to arrange it. He wanted to focus his full attention on Alyssa. Confirmation came a couple of seconds later. And, after glancing at his screen, another warning from Liz. Yes, caring for his ex while she was pregnant and vulnerable was a slippery slope. He was going into the situation with his eyes open, though. He told her to trust him when he said his heart couldn't take another hit like the one he'd taken when she walked out.

"Mind if I take a look at the paper?" he asked once he received confirmation from Liz that Dr. Samantha Brendan was on her way. Good. She was one of his favorite ER docs.

Alyssa studied him for a long moment. "Are you absolutely certain you want to get involved in this?"

"I am here, aren't I?"

"Not willingly. I showed up on your doorstep thinking that I couldn't wait to see my husband. You didn't sign up for this so much as have it thrown at you." The vulnerability in her voice threatened to crack some of the dam he'd constructed. Since he wasn't a fan of waterboarding, which was exactly what this would amount to should the dam break, he reminded himself to keep his distance. To bring home the fact, he took a seat across the coffee table from her, putting a solid five feet of mass between them.

"True. I won't deny you showing up here unexpected and in your condition after all these months has thrown me for a loop." He leaned forward, clasped his hands and rested his elbows on his knees. "But you're here. I'd like to think you showed up for a reason, like you're in trouble and you trusted me to help. In my job, I'm trained to put my personal feelings aside so I can focus on finding solutions. I'm also trained to be objective." She started to put up an argument, so he added, "Which doesn't exactly work in this case. Not a hundred percent. We have history that can't be ignored. I can get there."

Reading Alyssa had become next to impossible as she sat there, staring at the coffee table.

"I'll agree that I came here for a reason. I thought we were still married and the only reason I wasn't wearing my ring was because those jerks stole it." She didn't look up when she spoke.

"Again, true. You're here now. You're pregnant. Your instincts led you to my doorstep because despite anything else going on between us, you realized you could trust me."

"So, why do I feel like I'm putting you in danger by my presence?"

A piece of his heart and bruised ego wanted to believe that was true. That the reason she'd walked out eight months ago was because she was trying to protect him in some way. Yet, his practical "cop" side—the part of him that distrusted everyone and everything until they proved he could do otherwise—couldn't quite get there. It said she came back to use him only for protection. It suspected she was using him now as cover. It accused her of toying with his emotions to throw him off balance.

To what end? That was the question. As far as he

could tell, she had nothing to gain by being here. She hadn't asked for any money in the divorce, despite the fact his family had more than they could spend in a lifetime or two. Probably even more with compound interest. Point being, if she'd wanted something from him, she would have asked for it in the divorce.

Plus, she ran her own business with her father before he passed away. Their import business brought in pottery, handmade jewelry and knickknacks from Mexico. After he died and she took over, she changed. Blake had chalked up the difference in her to grief. Now that his father was gone, he knew something about losing a beloved family member. Blake was trying to finish the year on the job, so he could bow out and take his place in the family cattle ranching business.

Alyssa had been studying him the whole time he'd been in la-la land, deep in his own thoughts. She scooted up where she could reach the coffee table and then smoothed out the piece of paper against the solid wood.

"This is what I remember so far. If I'm honest, I don't know if this is real or some of it's imagined. That's just where I'm at." She shrugged. "So, I wasn't quite ready to share information yet."

"What you have here could be the difference between cracking the case wide open and them getting off the hook."

"It could also lead an investigation down the

wrong path. What if I'm mixing up details? What if I implicate the wrong person?" She had always cared about doing the right thing, which surprised him even more when she left him the way she did. He thought he knew the person he married.

"Any investigator worth his or her salt will take your head injury into account." He moved forward so he could see the page. "Take the pregnant girlfriend, for instance. If we have two guys, and one of those guys has a pregnant girlfriend, we know to look at him more closely. It doesn't condemn anyone. We follow the evidence to find the perp. Always. There are only so many resources and we need to concentrate those on the most likely candidate."

She pressed her lips together, forming a seam. It was one of dozens of little habits or giveaways a person noticed about their spouse and meant she was seriously considering his words.

"Everything I remember so far is on the paper. It isn't much."

"Sometimes the seemingly smallest detail can blow a case wide open. We caught a guy once because a robbery suspect was always described as having a blue tongue."

Her face screwed up. "How is that possible? Like a Chow Chow?"

"You know, like from eating candy. Either sucking on a blue raspberry sucker or one of those candies you dip in powder?"

"What are those called? Something-pop? I used

to love getting those for Halloween." Recognition dawned, creating a lively spark in her eyes. Her expression was a mix of unbridled excitement. He'd quashed it by telling her to slow down and keep her distance.

"Just like those. Thing is, he always wore a ski mask so no one could get a good look at his face. When he spoke, though, the tongue gave him away. We nicknamed him Blue Man Group. We had a suspect in custody at the time. But Handler—" he flashed eyes at her "—you remember Davis."

She nodded.

"He's on a routine traffic stop and realizes he's talking to someone with a blue tongue who, once he got out of his vehicle, fit the height and weight of the perp we're looking for."

"Which isn't enough to get the guy arrested," she surmised.

"No, it isn't."

"How'd Handler get him?" she asked.

"He knew enough to keep looking for evidence. As he scanned the back seat, he saw a black duffel bag. It had blended in with the interior of the guy's vehicle before, so Handler didn't pick up on it right away. Handler asked what was in the bag. The guy beat feet, Handler chased, and then had probable cause to search the vehicle."

"I'm guessing he had all the tools for a job in that duffel," she said.

"That and enough weapons in the trunk to arm

a small militia. Handler got the arrest and we got a dangerous criminal off the street."

She nodded and half smiled. "I see what you're doing here."

"Did it work?" He wanted to make her feel better about letting him see the paper. Trust was too much to ask for. She hadn't trusted him enough to talk to him before walking out the door, so he knew there was no trust between them.

THE DOORBELL RANG, causing Alyssa to jump. She clutched her chest in an attempt to calm her racing heart. All this excitement couldn't be good for the baby and she was suddenly grateful that Blake had forced the issue of her seeing a doctor. It would most likely bring peace of mind, and that was on short supply lately since waking up from the nightmare.

Blake shot a sympathetic look as he stood up and then answered the door. "Thank you for coming on such short notice, Dr. Brendan."

"We're not at the hospital. Call me Samantha."

Blake stepped aside after the greeting and Alyssa pushed to standing as the doctor stepped in the front door.

"Please, don't get up. Stay comfortable." Dr. Brendan was tall, blond and had what most would consider a knockout figure. Alyssa loved being pregnant. Feeling the little bean grow inside her was the greatest feeling ever. In this moment, however, the round belly and swollen ankles weren't feeling so hot when she compared herself to the perfectly fit, mid-to-late-thirties doctor.

"Thank you, Doctor." She tumbled on the way down, landing hard on her backside, grateful for the soft cushions of the sofa to catch her fall. Very graceful. Then again, being graceful wasn't exactly her forte since becoming pregnant. Everything felt off. Her balance. Her emotions. Her sense of gravity.

Blake was by her side in a heartbeat, looking like he didn't know if he should even attempt to help her.

"I'm fine. Just a little clumsy." Thankfully, embarrassment couldn't kill her, or she'd be dead. A red blush climbed up her neck, she could feel the trail of warmth that eventually gathered in her cheeks.

"Can I help?" Blake asked the doctor, who had her stethoscope out and was already kneeling next to Alyssa.

"I'll just be a few minutes," the doctor said after introducing herself to Alyssa. This close, it was easy to see Samantha Brendan's beautiful clear blue eyes. She had the whole blond and beautiful bit down pat.

It was petty for Alyssa to be jealous of a beautiful woman knowing her ex-husband well enough to be willing to make a house call. Except her heart didn't get the memo. It fisted at the thought of Blake being close with another woman on any level other than friendship or work colleague.

Calming down would be good. Jealousy had reared its ugly head with Liz and now with the doctor. Alyssa needed to relax, which, under the circumstances, felt next to impossible. There was so much she wanted to know.

The doctor performed a routine-enough exam, shining a small light in Alyssa's eyes, taking her pulse, and then blood pressure. Dr. Brendan then wrapped her stethoscope around the back of her neck and took a seat on the solid oak coffee table.

"Can you tell me what day it is?" she asked.

"Thursday, but I already asked."

"It's good that you remember." Despite not wanting to like the doctor, Alyssa did. The woman had kind eyes and a warm smile. "Were you injured?"

"My head." She reached up to the tender spot, refusing to poke at it. "I must've taken a blow to the head."

"Mind if I take a look?"

Alyssa sucked in a breath. "Go ahead."

The doctor stood and had Alyssa lean forward. Movement made her woozy and she felt the effects of adrenaline having completely faded. Exhaustion settled into her bones and for the first time since arriving she felt tired. *Weary* might be a better word. Like she could barely hold her head up. A full stomach and a safe place allowed her to relax.

Dr. Brendan felt around the bump. Alyssa winced with contact.

"Sorry. I know this is tender."

Tender was a good word. In that moment, it made Alyssa think of chicken. Chicken tenders. So, that's where she was on the tired scale. She was becoming silly.

Thankfully, the doctor returned to her spot.

"I'd like to clean up the wound. Doesn't look like you need stitches, so that's the good news. The bad news is it's going to hurt before it feels better."

"Okay."

True to her word, whatever she used to clean the area stung. In a few minutes, the work was completed, and the doctor returned to her spot while Blake stood in the background, feet apart in an athletic stance. His arms were folded across a broad chest—a chest she used to curl against when they watched a movie…

Reliving a past she couldn't remember didn't seem like a productive way to spend her time. Instead of going down that road, she redirected and instead focused on the doctor.

"Has the baby been moving?" Samantha asked.

"Yes." Alyssa realized her hands came up to cradle her bump when the doctor mentioned the baby.

"Have you had any cramping or bleeding?" Dr. Brendan asked.

"No bleeding. I had cramping a little while ago. It was the reason Blake called."

The doctor nodded. "Any other pain?"

"None. Other than the bruises hurting and me feeling like I could fall asleep sitting here, I think I'm okay."

"Any nausea or vomiting?"

"Nothing." She threw her hands up.

"Good. I'd say everything seems like it's still on track with you and the baby. May I listen to the baby's heartbeat?" she asked.

"Yes."

The doctor pulled her stethoscope from around her neck and replaced the earpieces. "Sorry if this is cold."

She rubbed the metal end before placing it on Alyssa's exposed stomach.

"Strong heartbeat." Dr. Brendan smiled. "Do you know if it's a girl or boy?"

"Girl."

Blake sucked in a burst of air.

"All good news here." The doctor smiled. She nodded before turning to look at Blake. "Everything is looking good so far."

The expression on his face was unreadable as he turned and walked out of the room.

"I can't seem to remember what happened in the past eight months. A lot of my recent memories are wiped out. The past few days are a complete blank. I didn't know I was divorced. I can tell you my name and where I live but I have no idea what day it is. Why is that?"

"Your head injury is most likely responsible for the selective memory loss. I also wouldn't count out the trauma you've been under. Combine the two and—" she shrugged "—this is where it becomes a gray area in medicine. I wish I had a more definitive answer. The good news is you're young and healthy and could hold on to memories that are closest to your heart."

"Does that mean I won't ever remember what happened?"

"No. It's likely you'll get pieces here and there. Bits that start to make more sense as other pieces come to you."

"Like filling out a jigsaw puzzle?"

"That's right. The more you try to force these things, the longer it usually takes."

Alyssa figured as much. The attempts she'd made so far resulted in accomplishing no more than a headache.

"Give it time. You're young and in excellent health."

Time. Did she have time? As it was, she felt like the guys responsible were getting away. They could be long gone by now, never to return to this area. If she had been caught up in a criminal network, they could send someone else for her. The thought Alyssa might never be safe again sent fire swirling around in her chest. There was no end to which she wouldn't go to keep her daughter safe.

Arms folded across his chest, Blake stepped inside the room and leaned against the wall.

"I'd like you to follow up with your OB as soon as possible." After gathering up her belongings, the doctor said, "I can see myself out."

"Thank you for coming by," Blake said.

The day was catching up to Alyssa and since Blake didn't seem in the mood for conversation she curled up on her side and hugged a pillow.

The questions she'd seen brewing behind his eyes would come soon enough.

Chapter Six

Blake rinsed the last of the plates before loading the dishwasher. He glanced up to see that Alyssa had curled up on the couch after the doctor left. His gaze traveled over her, stopping on her belly. A daughter? Blake couldn't begin to process what that might mean or how it would change his life except to say his protective instincts were already kicking into high gear. Shoving those thoughts aside, he called in sick to work and polished off the rest of the pizza, trying not to think too much about the strange twist of fate that brought his pregnant ex-wife back to his doorstep.

Since his shoulders were strung tighter than an overstrung cello, he figured a workout would allow him to think more clearly while he waited for word from Liz.

Forty-five minutes later, he showered, drank a protein shake, and then settled in with his laptop. Earbuds in one side, he watched a replay of one of his favorite football games, which always helped him clear his mind when he was overthinking a situation or case. He didn't want to know how many hours he'd spent working out and watching football in the weeks after Alyssa left. Liz was right. He'd been gutted.

Was she cold? He got up and walked toward her, grabbing a throw blanket on the way. The minute he placed it over her, she shot up. She curled her legs up and grabbed the blanket to cover herself. She sucked in a burst of air.

"Get away from me." Her gaze was unfocused, and he could tell she wasn't seeing him. Was she still half asleep?

"You're okay," he soothed. "It's me. Blake. You're home. No one is going to hurt you here."

Relief washed over her as she curled onto her side and immediately went back to sleep. The look of shock on her face was a gut punch he wouldn't soon forget.

Damn. Damn. Damn.

Blake reclaimed his seat at the table. Staring at the screen, he tried to shove the disturbing and confusing thoughts aside and enjoy the game. The image of her locked in a small closet churned in his mind. Then, there was the blow to her head. How had that happened? Had someone crept up on her from behind? Why didn't someone see it? Where was she when it happened?

It was dark outside before Alyssa stirred again. This time, she stretched and yawned. He'd tried to give the situation a rest while she slept but it proved impossible. There were too many questions whirling around in his head for him to settle down enough to concentrate on the game let alone enjoy it.

"How long was I asleep?" She yawned and stretched out her long legs. This was the complete opposite of when she'd been startled awake. He'd barely touched her with the blanket when she'd withdrawn like a snake recoiling before a bite.

"A couple of hours."

"Oh. Wow. Okay. It felt like a lot more." She rubbed her eyes and then stretched her arms out.

"Are you hungry?"

"I could eat." Her quick response told him she was starving.

He went to the kitchen and retrieved the food he'd ordered while she was asleep. "I had carne asada delivered from the Tex-Mex place you love. Or at least you used to."

"Yeah. I haven't had food from there since the last time we went."

Eight months and one week to be exact. Although, he didn't think this was the time to point the fact out to her. One minute he thought everything was fine. The next, she'd packed up and left while he was at work. The Dear John letter had been taped to the first place he hit after every shift, the fridge.

Blake shoved those thoughts aside as he walked into the kitchen. He pulled the covered plates out of the fridge and heated them, one at a time, in the microwave. Grabbing a TV tray on his way out, he set up a spot for her right where she sat. He grabbed her favorite flavored water from the cupboard and poured it over a glass with ice.

"When did you start drinking this? You hate water that fizzes," she stated as he set the glass down.

"I didn't. And I still do."

"Oh." That one word was loaded. And, no, he didn't feel like explaining that he couldn't toss out the orange-flavored fizzle water out of nostalgia, or that he maybe hadn't completely gotten over losing her, or some ridiculous hope he'd clung to far longer than he should admit that she would come home.

So, he settled on, "I forgot it was in there until just now."

"Oh." Again, there was more meaning in that one word than if she'd strung together an entire paragraph.

His comment was partially true. And, no, he wasn't being his best self by making it.

After settling in the same room but the opposite sofa, he asked, "Did you ask the doctor about your memory?"

"Yes."

"Did she say when you can expect it to return?" After the way she left, he couldn't for the life of him figure out why this was the first place she thought to come.

"It's tricky. There's no one-size-fits-all for head

injuries. Some of the reason I could have forgotten is the emotional trauma. The good news is that she did say at least parts of it should return."

"That's good for the case." He looked up in time to see the disappointment in her expression. "What do you expect, Alyssa? You divorced me. Remember?"

She nodded. "I mean, I don't remember actually, but I believe you when you tell me it was my decision. Although, I can't for the life of me figure out why."

"Not just a decision, but one you made without consulting me or giving me a real reason." He wasn't trying to rile her up, so he cut himself off right there before he really said something he'd regret.

"Oh."

He issued a sharp sigh. "What else did she say?" He figured the easy answer was that he was in law enforcement and she needed protecting, plus she most likely felt safe with him.

She shook her head, but he could see in her eyes that there was more to the story.

"Come on, Alyssa. I'm done with the secrets. If you want my help, you have to answer my questions honestly."

Her gaze came up and locked on to his. "I could be holding on to the memories that are the dearest to my heart."

Well, didn't that shut him up. Talk about feeling two inches tall. Someone needed to brand him with the word *jerk* on his forehead.

"Hey, look, I didn't mean—"

"No. Don't. I'm going to stop you right there. I don't remember what happened between us or why I felt the need to leave you like I did. The fact I *can't* remember doesn't mean I hurt you any less. I can only apologize for my past actions, Blake. I can't go back and change them. I can't in my right mind believe that I would leave a marriage after finding out that I'm pregnant. All my instincts had me running toward you, not away. So, I'm just as confused as you are. But I don't blame you for being angry with me. Hell, I'm mad at me for leaving a marriage I couldn't wait to come home to."

Blake heard everything she was saying. *This* sounded like the Alyssa he once knew and fell in love with. The other one existed too. The one who had the power to rip his heart from his chest.

"It just dawned on me that you didn't ask the doctor for a paternity test." Shock raised her voice a couple of octaves.

"Nope."

"Can I ask why?" She cocked an eyebrow.

"Putting the guys who tried to hurt you behind bars is my number one priority right now. You getting your memory back is a close second. Anything beyond that is a distraction." His cold words seemed to bounce off her. There was no way he was going down the road of thinking about becoming a father.

"That's fair." Her chin came up and out, a defensive move he'd seen her do before. "Now, can I ask a question?"

"Go ahead."

"Why do *you* think I left?"

Chapter Seven

"Your father."

A stab of pain pierced Alyssa's heart at the mention of her dad. How could she have forgotten the fact that he passed away? Was this how selective memory worked? Had she tucked away anything and everything that hurt to think about? It didn't explain why his death would have caused a split between her and Blake, though.

"His death?" she asked, hoping for more clarification.

Blake nodded.

"It just seemed like a wall came up between us after your father died. At first, you leaned into me more. Then, something changed. You stopped talking to me. You started staying at the office later and later." He took a bite of food and then chewed. "I thought you needed space."

"And you gave it to me." Of course he did. One thing stood out in her memories. Blake had been an attentive husband. For the life of her, she couldn't think of one reason why she would have pushed him away. She didn't recall his attention smothering her in any way. In fact, it had been exactly what she needed, when she needed it.

"You seemed to have a handle on what you wanted from me at the time," he admitted, quickly covering the hint of regret in his tone.

"But that's not what you think in hindsight?"

"I'm not so sure I did the right thing. My instincts back then had been to be there for you more. Instead, I buried myself in my work and told myself I was giving you space." A momentary look of regret darkened his features. His plate suddenly became interesting as he jabbed his fork into his steak burrito. Rather than take a bite, he pushed the food around on his plate.

"Do I still have a job?" Strange that she'd blocked out her work history.

"As far as I know. You inherited the family business from your father, so unless you sold it someone has to be running things. My guess is that person is you."

"Could someone have taken me to extort money from the company?" She wanted to swing by the office and see what kind of reaction she'd get. Was this the right time to surface? Were those men or others just like them out there waiting for her? Looking for the right opportunity to pounce?

"It's possible. From my understanding the business wasn't raking in a ton of money." He shrugged.

"I got the impression you were basically donating your time to keep your father afloat before he passed away. But then…" He flashed his eyes at her before finishing the sentence. He seemed to think better of saying what was on his mind when he took another bite of food instead.

She decided it might be better to walk away from that one. If it was important, the subject would come up again.

"Think it's safe to go to the office tonight? Poke around in my files?"

"We can. I can even arrange a police escort to your home…apartment?"

She shrugged. "Maybe we'll find a home address for me at the office. I must have blocked out my new place along with the other memories."

His cell buzzed. He looked around for it and then located it on the table. He pushed the tray away and almost knocked his plate off. His recovery displayed his athletic grace. He swooped the plate in his free hand while righting the tray with his other. Somehow, he managed to keep the fork from being catapulted across the room and nailing the opposite wall.

"Not bad, O'Connor," she remarked, smiling.

"They didn't call me Blake Hustle on the court for nothing."

This time, her smile was genuine. For a split second, the barriers between them dropped and they resumed the easy way they had with each other. Of course, the bedroom had been a different story.

There, they had more chemistry than a science lab. And since thinking about it was as productive as trying to get milk out of an orange, she forced her thoughts back to the buzzing cell phone.

Blake stood at the table as he answered. "Hey, Liz."

Hearing the name caused Alyssa's muscles to tense. One, for the attraction she was certain she felt on Liz's part with Blake. Alyssa had witnessed it while the two were partners even though Blake honestly couldn't pick up on it. He'd said partners always kidded around with each other. In her heart of hearts, she believed he saw it that way. Alyssa wasn't so confident about Liz's intentions. The second reason was that Liz was most likely calling with an update on the case.

Alyssa was still trying to wrap her mind around Blake's comments about his priorities right now. Was he avoiding the possibility of becoming a father? She might not remember much about the past eight months, but she was certain Blake was the father of her child.

He said a few uh-huhs into the phone, followed by an *I see.* He thanked Liz for the heads-up, and then ended the call.

"She said there were a few fibers and hairs collected from your clothing. They'll send them off to the lab." He shot a warning look as he reclaimed his seat. "Before you get too hopeful, getting results back from those can take weeks if not months. Investigations in the real world aren't anything like TV shows where results come back in a matter of hours. Liz is owed a favor, so she called in a marker. But it still might take weeks to hear anything."

"That's disheartening."

"I know," he agreed. "She was able to track your cell phone records. The last activity on your phone was three days ago. You made a call to an obstetrician by the name of Dr. Kero."

"Oh, right. I'm on weekly appointments now. I keep everything on my phone, including my calendar."

"It would be easy for someone to figure out your doctor appointments," he said.

"One of the jerks had a late-term girlfriend. The one I call Gruff for lack of a better word. He mentioned that he would have a hard time breaking or cutting off my finger to get me to talk because of the pregnancy. His girlfriend must be close to as far along as I am."

"Which means he would have an idea how often your appointments were. Do they schedule them at basically the same time every week?"

"Mine does. I mean, if I'm remembering correctly, I kept my appointments routine. As long as nothing came up, I got the same schedule every week." She gasped. "Could his girlfriend be a patient of Dr. Kero?"

"Liz will check into it. See how many other patients they have in the practice as far along as you are. Are there a lot of doctors in the practice? Is it a team?"

She shook her head. "No. Just Dr. Kero. I picked her because I didn't want to see someone new every week at the end of my pregnancy or risk a different doctor showing up last minute to deliver my daughter."

A look passed behind his eyes at the mention of the word *daughter* that she couldn't quite pinpoint.

"Do you remember anyone in the waiting room at the same time as you that could have been as far along as you?"

"I'm blurry on all that. I'm doing well to remember my doctor's name at this point." She figured Dr. Kero must be a positive person in her life or she would have selectively forgotten the doctor. Then again, she'd meticulously vetted the person who would care for her unborn baby. If she was going to go through the pregnancy and birth alone, she would need the best possible support team.

Hold on. Did she just remember making the decision to go it alone? Something felt off with that line of thinking. Or did she feel like she didn't have a choice? It was plausible she *believed* she had to go through it alone. Blake was clearly shocked by the pregnancy. Why wouldn't she have told him the minute she found out? Didn't he want children?

She remembered a vague conversation about him wanting to start a family later rather than sooner. He'd said he wanted to do something first.

What was it, though?

No. She was remembering it wrong. He'd said he *needed* to do something first. Big difference.

BASED ON LIZ'S INFORMATION, the last time Alyssa had her phone was three days ago. Had she been locked inside the closet the entire time? Or transported around to cut down on the heat? In the first twenty-four hours after an abduction with some of the known criminal elements in Houston, a victim was moved around two or three times. In part, to make it more difficult to track them but also to confuse the victims and make it more difficult for them to get their bearings.

The thought his child, if she was his and he wasn't quite ready to concede the point yet, had been abducted and possibly injured sent a well of anger shooting through him he never knew could exist.

"When should we head out to my office?"

"We need to take a minute before we act. I don't want to move you until I absolutely know it's safe." He was still surprised by his reaction.

"What should we do in the meantime?" She'd never been one to sit still. But that's exactly what this situation called for.

"Practice patience."

She shot him a look that said more than he needed to know of what she thought about his comment. When she took in a sharp breath, he figured he was about to be read the riot act. Instead, she blew it out slowly like she was doing some kind of yoga breathing.

"Talk to me about something familiar. Like… how's your family?"

Blake compressed his lips. His father's death was a little too raw. "They're doing the best they can under the circumstances."

"What happened, Blake?" The genuine concern in her voice tugged at his heart and threatened his carefully constructed defenses. There was no way he would allow those walls to come down. Not even with a stick of dynamite.

"On the good side, a few of my brothers are married now. Cash married a wonderful single mother. Renee and Abby seem to make him happy in a way I've never seen before." He'd felt it once with Alyssa but questioned whether any part of their relationship was real. "Then, there's Dawson who is now married to Summer. Those two are made for each other."

"I thought your brother was still unhappy about his divorce from someone named Autumn." Her eyebrows did that thing again. The thing they did when she was confused.

"Yeah, so, turns out she has a twin sister. Autumn was in trouble and her sister, Summer, tracked her down. She met Dawson and the two fell in love while finding out what happened to her sister. My brother was never this happy or in love. I can attest to that."

"He deserves it. All of your brothers do. They're all amazing people who should have the happiest lives." She'd gotten along with his family perfectly. Too perfectly? Was everything about Blake's life with his wife too perfect?

Right up until the day she took off.

"Tell me about your parents. I hope I'm not out of line in saying how much I miss talking to them." His expression must've dropped because she brought her hand up to cover her mouth. "Oh no. What happened?"

"My dad…" Blake had to stop right there. Talking about his father gutted him. Blake had looked up to Finn O'Connor as the strongest man alive. His father was honest, no one worked harder and he was the most down-to-earth soul who ever lived.

"Oh, Blake. I'm so sorry. What happened?" Alyssa was to her feet and then standing in front of him in a matter of seconds. She put her hand up to the center of his chest and then pressed her flat palm against his heart.

"He opened the investigation into my sister's disappearance, and someone came after him. We found him on the property." He dropped his gaze. "He'd been murdered."

"That's awful and scary."

Temporarily caught up in an emotional storm, he covered her hand with his. Hers was small by comparison. Delicate. Although, he wouldn't describe her as a wilting flower. Her femininity and strength made her even more beautiful in his book. There was something vulnerable about the way she was looking up at him now, something that connected to a place deep in his soul. It was like time warped and he got trapped in the wave—a wave that made the past eight months disappear.

Suddenly, the moment happening between them was the most intimate he'd ever felt with her. Rather than ride the horse until it broke, he stepped back and broke off contact.

"Your mother must be beside herself," she said quietly.

"Yes. She's also strong and has plenty of support. She'll get through it even though she seems a little bit lost without Dad."

"Of course, she does."

"It seems to help that there have been new faces coming into the family recently. Cash married a wonderful single mother and Dawson found his match with Summer."

"No one will ever replace Finn O'Connor. But I'm sure having new life around brings a whole different energy to the house."

He nodded. Emotion caught in his throat.

"I'm truly sorry, Blake. Losing your father is big and I hate that you had to go through it alone."

"I didn't." The words came out a little too harshly, but she needed to know he was fine.

They had the intended effect. She got so quiet he could hear a pin drop. So, why did that make him feel like a jerk?

He didn't want to feel the connection with her that

he'd once felt so strongly it seemed unbreakable, no matter how temporary. Liz was right. Going down the road of being close again wasn't an option. Not in his book. The two of them would have to come up with a custody, financial and visitation plan should the baby she was carrying turn out to be his child. There would be enough on their plates without adding the complication of emotions. He needed to apply his professional habits to home before this "connection" got out too far in front of him to reel it back in.

More than anything, he needed to lean forward in the saddle so the horse would back up a few steps.

Chapter Eight

The hurt Alyssa felt was temporary. Rejection always stung. Why she needed to remind herself of the fact now was beyond her. Hearing about the loss of Finn O'Connor had knocked her off balance. The fact he'd been murdered and found on the property sent an icy chill racing down her spine. Her baby was going to miss out on one helluva grandfather. Such a shame.

But the thought of splitting custody and seeing her daughter every other Christmas practically gutted her. The O'Connors had every right to be in her daughter's life. The realization that this was going to be harder than she originally expected nailed her. Was that the reason she'd kept her pregnancy a secret?

Blake was right about one thing. Focusing on the pregnancy and the complication of their relationship had to take a back seat to the investigation. So, she forced herself to think back to what they'd been talking about before she asked after his family.

The doctor's office. Other pregnant women who

were as far along as she was. Since Gruff had a distinct voice, she wondered if she could just call the office and ask the receptionist. On second thought, HIPAA laws made getting patient information next to impossible. Liz would have to badge her way to the data. An ordinary citizen couldn't get the information out of the front office. Not without some finesse. She'd have to think of a lead-in question. The office was probably closed for the evening, so that would give her some time to think about it.

Basically, they were at a stalemate until Blake thought it was safe enough to head into her office. Lucky for her, he could call in a few favors and have the area watched as they made the trip in. Having people who got paid to notice things would definitely be a good thing, especially if Nasal or Gruff was watching her office. The thought caused a chill to race down her spine. Three days. She'd been trapped in the trailer or something very much like it for seventy-two hours, give or take. The selective memory theory combined with a head injury easily explained her forgetfulness.

Before she could move on from the topic of his family, she had to add, "Your mom is an amazing person and so are your brothers."

He made a face and she knew exactly who he was thinking about. Garrett.

"I'm sure Garrett has good reasons for pushing everyone away," she argued. His brother was the rebel, the lone wolf of the family who didn't fit into the O'Connor family mold. "My point is that I'm still sorry for the family's loss. My heart goes out to each and every one of you. I know how much you loved and respected your father, Blake. I hate that he's gone so young."

Blake sighed. "Thank you. On behalf of my family, we appreciate your kindness."

His voice was stiff, and his words carefully chosen. It wasn't so much a hit against her as it was him struggling to keep his emotions in check. He'd always concealed his true feelings, except when it came to their relationship. She was beginning to realize how special it had been. How special it was for him to open up to her. And from a very deep place inside her, she ached.

A few minutes of silence passed after the two reclaimed their seats in the living room. She picked up her piece of paper along the way. Once seated and comfortable, which was saying a lot at this stage of pregnancy, she closed her eyes and let her mind wander. She strained to hear Gruff's voice, once again remembering he was the more compassionate one of the pair. The thought that he and his partner could be out there searching for her or kidnapping another person fueled her desire to recall.

Random thoughts drifted in and out. Attempting to discipline her thoughts was laughable. No matter how much she tried to concentrate, the most random things popped into her mind. Like, watermelon. And how good dinner was. This was a treat, a meal when they were both too tired to cook. Why was she tired? Working a lot of hours. Remembering her father as he lay in bed, too sick to lift a fork to his mouth. Pneumonia. He'd been too weak to fight it. Both she and Blake were fatherless now. What a strange thought to have lost both of their fathers in the span of less than a year.

"Everything okay?"

"Yes." She opened her eyes. "My mind is wandering despite my best efforts to try to remember."

"It'll come back." His tone held more compassion now and she wondered if he'd snapped into cop mode. He would get more out of a witness if he came across as sympathetic. He lowered his tone when he said, "Thank you for all the nice things you said about my family a minute ago. I'm still trying to process the fact that my father went to his grave without ever knowing what happened to Caroline."

Considering he was talking to her about something that mattered very much to his family, she wanted to make sure he knew she cared. Their marriage might not have lasted, but from a place deep inside her, she cared about him and his family. She still did. The emotion threatening to overwhelm her couldn't come from another place but love.

Strange that she still loved a husband she'd divorced.

"Is that why you're still working in Houston as a cop?" She hit the nail on the head when he compressed his lips.

"Figure I'll take my rightful place at the ranch soon enough. Everyone is circling the wagons to make sure someone is with Mother twenty-four-seven. We know that Dad was investigating Caroline's death when he was killed. Mother also revealed he was sick. Not something that would take him out right away, but over time he'd become sicker."

"I'm guessing that's the reason your father took up the investigation again."

"We're figuring the same. He knew his time was winding down. His condition would have taken years to bring him down, but he saw the end of the line and wanted closure." The first time she'd heard about Blake having a sister who'd been kidnapped from her crib in the family home while still an infant was on the drive to meet his family. Their relationship had obviously moved to the next level when he invited her to meet his folks. He'd mentioned something about Sunday supper and the whole family being around. He'd warned her they could be a lot to handle all at once but that he was one hundred percent certain his parents would love her.

From the minute she set foot on the O'Connor ranch, she'd been welcomed. The place in all its grandeur had caught her off guard. It was also the first time she realized Blake came from money. Lots of it. Boatloads. Despite being the most grounded person she'd ever met. Her father had always chased money like it was a deer and he had to hunt using only his hands. *Elusive* was a good word to describe his approach to money. They had enough. She had meals on the table and a mother who stayed at home to bring up children. Alyssa was supposed to be one of three or four, but her mother had had a complicated pregnancy and was unable to have more children.

"My mom depends on me for money," Alyssa blurted out. "I'm sorry. I didn't mean to change the subject like that. It just came to me."

"Really?"

"It's why I was working so hard to help my father. I'm sure of it." The fact this was news to him told her she hadn't confided in him before. Why?

"You might want to write it down on your paper." He motioned toward the piece in her hand.

She smoothed it out on the TV tray while he located the pen and then brought it to her. She wrote down *money problems?*

When money entered the picture, a whole different kind of motive came to mind. So, she wrote that word down too. *Greed.*

"IT'S ONE OF the top motives for murder." Blake realized her kidnappers had kept her alive instead.

"My finger. Gruff said something about having a hard time thinking about breaking or cutting off my finger to get me to talk. And they mentioned Bus Stop and Judge but I have no idea who they were referring to."

Greed could be a motivator for a kidnapping. Either for ransom, which seemed not to be the case here. Or to sell information.

Alyssa gasped. "I need to call my mother and tell her to go away for a few weeks."

Blake retrieved his phone and then handed it over.

She stared at it, blinking rapidly. "I don't have the first idea what the number is."

"Hold on." No one remembered phone numbers anymore. He pulled up her mother's contact in his phone.

"You kept this?" She said the words low and under her breath, but the hint of hope nearly did him in. He didn't want to give her false hope about where he stood.

"More like I never deleted it."

"Oh."

He was beginning to hate that word.

Alyssa took the cell from his hands, their fingers touched, and sparks flew where they made contact. He did what he did best—ignored them.

"Mom," Alyssa started right in, "where are you?"

A few beats passed.

"Can you go stay with a friend tonight?" she asked. Then came, "Pack a weekend bag. I might need you to…No, I can't explain right now. I'll tell you later. Okay?" More beats passed. "Will you trust me?"

Those words must have been magic because Alyssa nodded, and a ghost of a smile crossed her

lips. "Good. Thank you, Mom. I'll explain everything later."

She looked up at Blake, their eyes locked and his
heart fisted.

"Yes, this is Blake's phone and, in fact, he's standing here right now if you'd like to—"

She paused for a few beats.

"He'll understand. We just had to tie up a few
loose ends at the townhouse. Has anyone been by
lately?" she asked. "Good….No. Don't answer your
phone unless it's me or Blake calling. And don't answer the door if the bell rings. Just pack your bag…
What?…Yes…The baby and I are fine." A few more
beats of silence passed. "Nothing to worry about
here. Just take care of you and I'll come for you when
you can come home. Okay?"

She nodded and the smile returned, brightening
her creamy skin. Blake didn't want to think about
how beautiful his ex was. Seeing her pregnant, glow-
ing, she was even more stunning. Looks could get
a person only so far with Blake. Intelligence with a
sense of humor were high on his list. Kindness. Good
looks were icing on the cake.

The question he'd spent too many nights ponder-
ing returned—what had he done wrong?

"Remember that thing I was asking about the last
time we talked?" Alyssa asked. She must be fish-
ing for information from her mother. "Yeah, when
was that?"

She nodded and said a few uh-huhs into the phone.

"Well, get over to Annie's and enjoy your time with her," she finally said.

Alyssa ended the call with her mother looking satisfied. "She promised to text as soon as she gets to her friend Annie's house."

Getting Alyssa to the office she'd share with her father jumped up higher on the priority scale.

"What about where you live? Is it coming back to you?" he asked.

She shook her head.

"I might have something around here with your address on it." Would the divorce papers? He honestly couldn't remember. The whole time period was a blur and, honestly, he didn't want to recall most of it. But he had the papers somewhere upstairs in his home office.

"We could pull up the picture of your residence and see if it jogs any more memories."

There was Google Maps. He'd run upstairs and root around for papers he swore he'd never look at again once they were signed and the deal was done. Blake took the stairs two at a time. The master was on this level along with two other bedrooms, one of which he used as an office. The second bedroom was a guest room and several of his brothers had taken turns staying over to keep him company after he'd been served. The master had its own hallway while the bedroom and office were side-by-side.

He hiked down the hallway to the office and moved behind his desk. Then, he remembered the papers were most likely in the filing cabinet behind him. He pivoted and dropped down to one knee before opening the bottom drawer. In the back, he saw the folder marked Divorce. He'd swallowed a bitter pill with that one and the taste soured his mouth now just thinking about it.

The sealed envelope sat there where he tucked it away after being reassured by his attorney everything was signed and in order. The promise he'd made nullified by the words *irreconcilable differences*. What did that even mean?

He grabbed the envelope. On the way downstairs, he heard his cell buzzing. He picked up the pace. The call rolled into voicemail before he got there in time.

Alyssa met him at the bottom of the stairs, cell in one hand and his laptop tucked underneath her arm.

Again, when their fingers made contact the inconvenient attraction surged. This close, he could breathe in her scent, a mixture of lavender and spring flowers that brought all his senses to life. He hadn't made the time to toss out her favorite body wash.

"Here's your phone." Her voice was low and sexy. Her eyes were glittery. He recognized the look. Hell, he felt the same. Physical attraction had never been an issue for them even right up until the end.

Call him an idiot—and he had been for not recognizing the signs he was losing his wife—but he'd believed their healthy sex life meant they were clicking on all levels. She'd been distracted and different since her father's death. Quiet. Now, he realized the fact she'd stopped talking to him was a problem. *The* problem?

Having her show up now was good, he reasoned. Maybe now he'd be able to get closure. It was pure muscle memory that had him tucking the envelope under the same arm as the laptop as his phone stuck in between them. With his free hand, he started to take her by the wrist but brought his hand up to cup her cheek instead. The feel of her creamy skin against his hand sent rockets shooting through him.

It would be so easy to dip his head down and kiss those gorgeous pink lips of hers. He blamed his next actions on muscle memory when he did just that—kissed her. And her lips against his was even better than he remembered.

She tasted sweet and a little spicy, the lingering effects of Tex-Mex peppers as he teased his tongue inside her mouth. She parted her lips for him, and he drew out the sweetness of kissing his wife again. *Wife?*

The word was the equivalent of a bucket of ice being poured over his head. He pulled back enough to break apart. He rested his forehead on hers, wishing for a life that could never be.

After a few slow breaths to calm his racing heart, he said, "Thanks for bringing my phone to the stairs."

"Yeah. No problem." Her breath came out in rasps too. There was primal satisfaction in the knowledge he had the same effect on her as she had on him. It might be fleeting and for all the wrong reasons, but he enjoyed the fact that she was still attracted to him. Call it bruised ego.

He took the phone from her, needing to keep his hand busy anyway because it wanted to act on its own accord and touch her again. Glancing at the screen, he muttered a curse. Colton. His brother, the sheriff, had called. And there was a voicemail he didn't figure Alyssa needed to hear.

"You want to take these while I check on my brother and make sure he doesn't need anything this red-hot minute?"

"Um, sure."

"Feel free to open the envelope. I'm sure you got a copy, so you'll already know what is in—"

He caught himself right there and shot her a look of apology.

"It's okay. It's strange that I don't remember these last eight months. But I'm not surprised that I would block out the time I spent without you." Well, those words weren't going to help him keep a distance, physical or otherwise.

Since responding would only invite more trouble, he bit his lip to clamp his mouth shut and then handed over the laptop and envelope. He took in a breath as she moved to the kitchen table and cleared enough space for two people to sit there. He'd used it mostly as a place to stack everything from unimportant mail to folded clothes that never made it upstairs. Considering the laundry room was on the ground floor, he figured he was doing well by making it up at least one flight. Forget the fact a cleaning lady came in once a week and wasn't due to come until tomorrow.

Last thing he needed was more eyes inside the house or to put anyone else at risk while Alyssa was home. A guest, he corrected, not home.

Chapter Nine

Liz called. Call me back ASAP. That was the voice-mail in its entirety from Colton. His brother had found happiness with his new wife, Makena, and this worried tone had everything to do with Blake and not Colton's personal life.

Blake figured making this call was the equivalent of taking his medicine. He also reminded himself it wouldn't be a good idea to talk to Liz while he was ready to wring her neck. Did she have to bring his family into this?

First, he fired off a text to excuse the cleaning lady while he was still thinking about it, giving her the day off tomorrow with pay.

Then he returned his brother's call.

"Everything okay?" Colton skipped perfunctory greetings, which meant his level of concern was at DEFCON 2.

"Depends on your definition of the word. But, yes, I'm fine."

"What do you need from us? We want to help," Colton said.

"Nothing right now. Alyssa is here. She's staying the night in the guest room." He probably emphasized the last two words a little too much.

"I can be there in a couple of hours."

That wasn't exactly true. It would take more than a couple of hours to make the drive to Houston. "I appreciate the offer, but all is well here. Don't worry."

"I wasn't," Colton said quickly. Too quickly.

"Did Liz bring you up to speed?"

"She said your ex showed up at your door in trouble."

"Is that all?"

"In a nutshell."

Blake figured that was just enough to cause a three-alarm panic.

"I was hoping you could fill in the details for me."

"She doesn't remember anything," he started and then quickly told him what happened.

"I can check into similar reports being filed. See if there are any other cases even close to this."

"She mentioned one of the guys has a pregnant girlfriend." He wondered how much Liz shared with Colton about Alyssa's condition. "About eight months pregnant. Same as Alyssa."

Based on the silence coming through the line, Liz had left that part out. At least she'd given him the opportunity to break the news to his family. He would go a little easier on her for that.

In the silence, Colton had to be doing the math.

"She says the kid is mine, but, honestly, I can't think about that right now."

"Really?" Colton's shock caught Blake off guard. "It's a big thing to find out you might be a dad. Are you sure you want to shove that aside?"

Colton knew how people in law enforcement worked. Everything had a nice, neat box. Come up on a man beating his wife…emotions went into a box. Being rational kept the peace and made Blake a better officer. As a human, he wanted to take the guy out back and teach him what it was like to have someone bigger than him throw a punch, but that wasn't his job. His job was to be objective and keep the peace. There was no room for personal feelings. They got in the way and could be dangerous. They also made him less objective. Like the time when he witnessed a two-hundred-pound man put his hands up to a five-feet-four-inch woman. From Blake's angle, it looked like the guy was about to throw a punch. Blake calmly advised the man to put his hands down and then witnessed the woman smack the guy with the baseball bat she'd been hiding on the side of her leg out of Blake's view. He'd gone in hot, emotional and ready to save the smaller person who turned out to be the aggressor. The guy was trying to defend himself.

So, yeah, he'd learned to keep his emotions in check and observe before acting.

"The threat to Alyssa is real. Right now, I can't focus on anything else," he defended.

"I mean, yes, I understand that. But becoming a parent in... How far along did you say she was?"

"Eight months."

"In a matter of a few weeks, sooner if the baby comes early, isn't something easily put off." His brother's point was well taken.

"What do you suggest, Colton? I have no idea how to process becoming a father let alone the fact that my ex-wife didn't bother to tell me she was pregnant until the eleventh hour. I'm more concerned with making sure both of them live before I decide how to process the pregnancy. Plus, Alyssa doesn't remember leaving. She doesn't remember walking out or making sure I was served with divorce papers. And I don't know how I feel about her showing up here other than pissed." All those words just tumbled out of his mouth, unfiltered. Would he reel a few back in if he could? The obvious answer was a resounding hell yes. He couldn't, and damned if it didn't feel a little better to talk to someone.

Colton was quiet.

"Are you there?"

"Yes. Always." Those words reassured and Blake needed to hear them.

"So, what do you think? Are you going to give me a lecture about inviting Alyssa back into the house?" He didn't say *into his life* but they both knew that's what he meant.

"I think there's a lot of honor in what you're doing. Other than that, I'm just here for you in any capacity you need me to be. You want help with the investigation… I'm here. You want someone to listen to you vent… I'm here. You need company… I can be there in a few hours."

"What about advice?"

"Nope. I don't have any. I don't know enough about the situation to render an opinion worth salt. I was glad Liz called because she knew you wouldn't. And I'm here to tell you that you don't have to go through any of this alone."

"Alyssa showed up thinking we were still married. For a split second, I thought she was playing some kind of cruel joke, but no one could be that awful. The doctor mentioned selective memory and that she could have blocked out anything upsetting."

"I see." There was no judgment in Colton's response. In fact, he was being more understanding than Blake expected. That was the thing about being an O'Connor. The family knew how to rally around each other. He realized just how much he missed living on the ranch and being surrounded by family. His job in law enforcement wasn't providing the bird's-eye view he'd hoped for in figuring out what had happened to his sister all those years ago. Every trail was a dead end.

"There are some questions as to her family business. She remembers being financially responsible for her mother and feeling the weight of the burden since her father passed away. She ran the business with him and became fully responsible after his death."

"I'm guessing your next move is to take her to the office."

"As long as I can do it safely. I thought maybe taking her in the middle of the night with some of my buddies watching out for us would be the best route. There'd be fewer vehicles on the road, and it would be easier to spot someone trying to follow us."

"It would." There was a note of approval and a hint of pride in Colton's voice that reminded Blake of everything he'd been missing. The past eight months living alone had brought home just how stubborn he could be. He had a family to lean on but was too damn proud to ask for help. It was a lot like asking for directions. He had to first admit he didn't know where he was going. His pride had already taken a huge hit with the divorce—the ultimate sign he had no idea what he was doing in the most important area of his life. He still couldn't figure out how he'd been so dead wrong about someone.

"She isn't sure when she was last at work, for obvious reasons, so could you reach out on her behalf and find out if they're even missing her?" Blake asked.

"I'll dig around on my end. See what I can come up with."

"I'd appreciate it. I'll take all the help I can get on this one." He was done being stubborn and fighting the world on his own. "If Cash has time, I'd like him to get involved too. If a crime ring is involved, this could cross state and even country lines."

"How so?"

"The trailer she escaped from has all the earmarks of being used regularly for human trafficking. Liz is canvassing the neighbors to see what they know or what they've seen."

"If this operation is big, it might be tough to get people to speak out against it. It might help if she has something to bargain with."

"I'll have her run the witnesses. See if we can find any outstanding warrants." His brother brought up a good point. Walking into a crime ring with no bargaining power was about as smart as trying to trade a fish for a horse. It was a deal no one in their right mind would take. "I appreciate the advice."

"Any time. I'll bring in Cash and the others. See if anyone has information or resources that can help. In the meantime, be careful. And I don't just mean take care of her and the baby. Look over your own shoulder too." Their brothers Cash and Dawson worked for the US Marshals Service. Both would be great resources.

"Will do, Colton." Blake ended the call with the first feeling of hope he'd had in longer than he could remember. Going home to live and take his rightful place at the ranch just became a priority.

ALYSSA STARED AT the paper where she was making notes as a text came through that her mother was safe. At least she could breathe a little easier on that front. With one of her worries out of the way, she pushed up to standing. Frequent trips to the bathroom were becoming her new norm.

Blake opened the door as she stood, and then she cramped so hard she sat right back down. He was by her side before she hit the sofa. She doubled over and panic engulfed her.

"What can I do?" He'd never looked more helpless. Not even the time she was on the ranch with him while a calf was being born breech. After pacing a couple of rounds in the stall, he'd rolled up his sleeves, dropped to his knees and helped pulled out the little brown newborn calf while she'd stood there in shock. Alyssa was from Houston, born and raised in the city. She was by all accounts a city girl.

Remembering to breathe through the contraction, she waved him off as she focused on her breathing. When her birthing class teacher had told the group to breathe through a contraction, she'd almost laughed out loud. But then she'd looked up, and realized the teacher was serious. What? No miracle yoga pose? No shot of whiskey? No tree branch to bite down on?

Breathe?

Hadn't she been doing that her entire life? If getting rid of period cramps was as easy as breathing, wouldn't she have had the hang of it by now?

Okay, big whoop, the teacher had given them a breathing technique. The end result was the same, take in air—exhale. She'd walked out of class that night vowing never to return. She'd called Dr. Kero the following morning and told the office she wanted to revise her birthing plan. The whole "breathing" method to get rid of pain wasn't going to cut it. She'd told them to give her as many drugs through the delivery as was safe for the baby. Women might have birthed babies in between chores in the old days, but death rates were high, and now she had better *and* safer options for both her and the kiddo.

The whole he-he-he, ha-ha-ha trick she was doing now was working. So, yeah, she would be embarrassed later when this whole episode settled down.

"Are you in labor?" Blake finally asked when her he-he-he, ha-ha-ha bit settled down.

"Maybe we should time these. If another one comes, we panic."

Based on the wide-eyed, openmouthed response she got from Blake, that wasn't the answer he was expecting. He checked the clock on his phone anyway.

"It could be all the activity I've had. Your friend said the heartbeat was strong and the baby has been active in the last hour."

Blake nodded before taking a seat on the solid coffee table. He gave her a quick update on his conversation with his brother and let her know Colton was planning to touch base with her office to make sure no one was looking for her. He put his hands on his thighs and issued a sharp sigh. "I'm sorry you've been going through this pregnancy alone."

Now, it was her turn to be shocked. She expected

him to be mad as hell at her for not coming to him right away and telling him about the baby in the first place. Although, she'd blocked all of that out. She must've had her reasons despite not for the life of her being able to figure out what those might be now.

Studying Blake, she felt nothing but love, deep and enduring.

The next cramp didn't double her over. She definitely felt it, though. The pain wasn't on the same scale as the first. She used the breathing technique again. It worked. Basically, she owed an apology to one Lisa Waterson, baby birthing guru, and needed to withdraw her request for a refund for the class. Miss Lisa deserved a bonus. Once this ordeal was over, Alyssa needed to stop by with a gift card for her former teacher.

A few more rounds of cramping later, Blake announced the cramps were erratic.

"I think you should call your doctor anyway on the emergency line," he said.

"Better safe than sorry. I probably should have called already considering how far along I am. It's possible that I've missed a weekly appointment. My doctor could be frantic." She cradled her bump thinking how crazy it was for her to love someone she hadn't officially met yet. Feeling the little bean grow inside her, kicking and stretching, made Alyssa feel very attached. Seeing her sweet angelic face on 3-D sonograms made Alyssa even more eager to meet her daughter.

The pregnancy news had come as a shock. This was a real memory, not an assumption based on the present situation between her and Blake. "It took me a while to adjust to finding out I was pregnant."

"Yeah?" A brow arched. A question.

"It's a memory. I distinctly remember holding the stick and seeing two lines. I was in shock and confused. All I could think about was how to tell you." She cast her eyes down at the wood flooring. "Obviously, I didn't. I don't know why I wouldn't tell you when all I could think about when I woke up in that dark closet was getting home to you."

He brought his fingers up to her chin and lifted it so she was looking into his eyes. "You're here now. I know what's going on now. That's what matters."

And yet, there was a piece of her memory that was missing, which seemed to matter more than anything else: why had she walked away from him to begin with?

Chapter Ten

The genuine anguish in Alyssa's eyes stripped away a little more of Blake's defenses. Touching her was a bad idea, so he brought his hand back to his thigh. "You should probably make that call."

He waited as she called the after-hours line. She left a message for the nurse, who returned the call within minutes. For the first time since this whole ordeal had started, he let himself contemplate what it would mean to be a father. The first person who came to mind was Cash. His older brother was in the process of adopting his new wife's infant daughter. Cash had adapted to fatherhood so fast Blake's head was still spinning. And it looked like the most natural thing to see him hold Abby.

Did Blake want to have children? If the child turned out to be his, he wouldn't have much of a choice. He'd have to figure out fatherhood on the fly despite the fact kids weren't in his game plan. At least, not for now. His renewed vow to find out what had happened to Caroline was his priority. He didn't need anything or anyone distracting him from the promise he'd made to himself. The knowledge and justice his mother deserved.

Now, his father was dead after stirring the pot. With a baby on the way, would Blake be free to take the risks necessary to get to the truth?

He thought about his brothers who now had spouses and families. He might be a hypocrite, but he would tell them to back off the investigation if he thought it would do any good. Every O'Connor had his own cross to bear when it came to feeling the responsibility of finding out the truth.

Alyssa ended the call and Blake tuned back in.

"The nurse said everything sounded good since I don't have any bleeding. I missed my weekly appointment and didn't call in, so they want me to stop by tomorrow. They've been worried about me. I didn't know what to tell them, so I just redirected the conversation to the cramps." She shrugged. "I didn't know what else to say."

"What time do they want you to go in tomorrow?" He'd need to arrange an escort for them. Houston was a big city with serious crime, so he would call in a favor from an off-duty officer or two. If the kidnappers were somehow linked to her doctor's office, she might be walking right into their hands. Her family business was one thing. She could avoid going there unless the right circumstances presented themselves.

"Eleven o'clock."

"That will give me time to have Liz stop by the

office and see what she can find out." He was keeping Liz plenty busy. He would owe her one for all her help. "Instead of going into your office tonight, what do you think about staying here and putting your feet up?"

"I was just about to suggest the same thing." She blew out a frustrated-sounding breath.

"Patience wins battles," he said by way of reassurance.

"It's frustrating to have limitations. Don't get me wrong, I can't wait to meet this little girl and I have no doubt in my mind all of the sacrifices I'm making now will be worth it."

He clasped his hands together and listened.

"But not being able to go full speed when I want to make sure these guys are behind bars makes me want to scream sometimes."

"I hear what you're saying. You've been doing a great job of caring for...her. You have help now, so even though it feels like you're not doing anything, progress on the investigation is being made. You have to trust others to step up." He surprised himself with the bitterness that crept into his tone on the last part. Did she need to hear it? Probably not right now and he wasn't trying to be a jerk.

"I deserve that."

"No." He issued a sharp sigh. "You don't." Although he couldn't think of one good reason for her to keep the pregnancy from him, there had to have been something that had held her back. "Can I ask you one question, though?"

"Yes. I can't promise I'll know the answer." She folded her arms across her chest and rested them on top of her belly.

"Did you know about the baby before you left?"

"I can give you a definitive answer there. No. I found out about the pregnancy after. I'm solid on the fact." She was already gone and then found out she was pregnant.

"Did you have plans to tell me?"

"I wish I knew." She shrugged. "It's frustrating."

Since that was a dead-end road, he pivoted the conversation. Besides, it didn't make a difference. There was a baby involved. Blake would deal and do the right thing by the kid if it turned out to be his.

It was getting late and she would be more comfortable in bed.

"What do you think about trying to get some sleep?" His workout had done its job. His body could settle. Blake could go days without sleep if he needed to. Tonight, he would rest.

"This might sound crazy because I know I showered when I first got here. Another one would be heaven." She'd always showered before bed.

"Do you need help?" He caught how that sounded after the words left his mouth. "Don't take it the wrong way. I mean, help getting upstairs."

"I'll take all the help I can get right now."

"You know that I'm in this for the long haul, right?

I have no plans to walk away and leave you to bring up a child on your own if that's my daughter." He needed to be specific with her about his intentions.

"You want to hear something strange? That makes all kinds of warning bells sound off in my head. Like, that's somehow a bad thing." She pushed up to standing with some effort. "How messed up is that? Having a baby's father around—and especially someone as honorable as you—should be a good thing. Yet, it's literally sending panic vibes racing through my body."

Did that mean the baby wasn't his?

THE CONFUSED LOOK on Blake's face mirrored what was going on inside Alyssa's head. She knew, without a doubt, he was the baby's father. The thought was unshakeable in her mind.

"Are you afraid of me? Afraid that I would take the child away from you?" It was a valid question at this point. One she didn't have an answer to.

"In my heart, I don't believe so. Was there a fight between us before I left?"

"No." He held out an arm and she took the lifeline as she waddled toward the stairs.

"Can you remind me of our situation? Maybe it'll jog a memory. Were we happy?"

"No." There was so much resignation in his tone. "I thought we were okay. You started acting different after your father died."

"I know he died from pneumonia but had he been

sick a lot prior? Do we know what brought it on?" She honestly couldn't remember.

"It came on suddenly."

"Nothing else? No foul play, right?" she asked. Considering she'd been abducted, it seemed like a fair question.

"None that you mentioned. There was no police investigation. No obvious sign of foul play. Your father became ill and passed away from pneumonia in the hospital. He'd been a lifelong smoker and was having issues with emphysema. You were always on him about his smoking."

"That feels familiar." She paused. "You said the two of us weren't happy." She circled back to their relationship.

"There was a lot of distance between us. I thought we were fine and that we'd reconnect once you settled your father's affairs and got your mother situated." There was so much honesty in his eyes and sadness in his voice as he spoke.

"But I didn't."

"No." He shook his head. "And I should have talked to you. I should have kept talking until you couldn't take it anymore and started talking just to shut me up."

"You can't blame yourself for the breakup of our marriage. By all accounts, I did it."

"I let myself believe that for a long time, Alyssa. I did. I wanted it to be all your fault because you're the one who walked. But the truth is no relationship is carried by one person. And no relationship is broken by one person. I didn't do enough to let you know how important you were to me."

"I might have walked anyway, Blake." She couldn't imagine doing it the first time let alone if he'd put up a real fight.

"True. But I wouldn't be filled with all these *what if* questions." They crested the top of the stairwell. "What if I'd talked more? What if I didn't let you get away with being gone so much.? What if I'd taken leave from work to help you settle your father's affairs? What if I'd taken you back to the ranch like I wanted to?"

"Might have turned out the same."

"Then I would be able to let go of all this regret. As it is, I'll take it to my grave."

Those words were the equivalent of being stabbed in the center of the chest. "I wish there was a way to convince you none of this was your fault. I only remember you as being an amazing husband. Someone I couldn't wait to get home to."

"Your memories will come back, and you might think differently." Was that part of the reason the walls between them were thickening? One step forward. Two steps back.

There was no right way to respond. She could argue, but he might be right. She could agree and frustrate him more. There had to be a way to give him an out and release him from beating up on himself. She had to find a way to show him the blame was on her. For reasons she couldn't explain, she knew it had been her fault.

"Are you good from here?" he asked.

"Yes." She let go of his arm.

"You left more clothing behind than what was in the closet. The cleaning lady packed them in a box and put them in the guest closet. I can dig it out and find some of your old things for you to sleep in."

"I doubt any of my shirts would fit now."

"You can borrow one of mine. You have undergarments and some of your favorite yoga-type pants in there," he said.

"That would be nice." She didn't want to get too excited about the fact her clothing was still there after all these months. Had he hung on to them for sentimental reasons? Did she still have a place in his heart? Or had she ruined the best thing that had ever happened to her?

"I kept forgetting to take them downstairs so I could donate them." He started down the stairs. "Out of sight, out of mind."

All her hopes fizzled like a deflated balloon. Still, a nighttime shower was on the menu and she loved the relaxation that came with warm water sluicing over her. Her legs were tired. Heck, her bones were tired. And yet, she had no plans to shortchange her shower time.

Some of the ache eased while water pounded sore muscles. A knock on the door preceded Blake's voice letting her know he was putting some folded clothes on the counter for her.

Many of her favorite knickknacks were gone as well as most of the art she'd carefully selected. Had he boxed those pieces up or did she take them? An image popped into her thoughts of her grabbing a few of her things on a rainy night. She was in a hurry. Scared. She threw as much as she could into a pair of trunks and then loaded up her SUV. The only picture she'd taken with her was that of her wedding.

Driving away from the townhouse, tears streaming down her cheeks, she pictured herself saying goodbye.

A memory? Or a dream? Nightmare would be more like it.

Alyssa cut off the spigot before stepping out of the shower. She heard the click-click-clack of a keyboard from down the hall. The bathroom door was cracked, and she appreciated Blake's thoughtfulness. He probably wanted to be able to hear her should she need him.

On the counter sat her favorite pair of yoga pants. A George Strait concert shirt that was so worn in it wasn't funny was folded on top. The shirt might technically belong to Blake, but she'd claimed it during their marriage as hers.

She picked it up off the counter and held it to her cheek. It smelled clean, masculine and spicy, like campfires on a fall evening…like Blake. The cotton material was worn to silk. She breathed in the shirt one more time before putting it on. Her belly caused it to look like a tent, but she didn't care. It was so soft, and so Blake.

On top of her favorite yoga pants sat a pair of underwear. They fit and she'd take the win. Yoga pants were next. Those were stretchy enough to make work. She didn't realize how much she'd missed the comforts of home.

This was temporary, she reminded herself. Once the danger had been resolved, she would go back to her life and Blake would go back to his. She wanted to be able to help him with his sister's case in some way. Pay him back for everything he was doing for her right now. After the way she'd walked out on him, he was a saint for taking her in and she better understood his initial reaction when she'd shown up out of the blue.

A little piece of her wished life had turned out differently. That she still lived here, and they were excited about the baby. The guest room would make the perfect nursery. She could envision painting the room and decorating for the little angel on the way.

Blake was going to make an amazing father. Period. He had all the qualities their daughter would want in a dad. And Alyssa wanted their daughter to grow up frequently visiting his family's ranch. The childhood he'd described had been the best anyone could have hoped for under their tragic circumstances. The kidnapping of his sister haunted the family.

Alyssa cradled her bump. Had she been afraid their child would be abducted like Caroline? It was impossible. Right? The timeline of when she'd found out about the pregnancy was off. But with his father's death coming so soon after stirring the pot, she did have to consider her daughter's safety when it came to being an O'Connor.

She followed the sound of the keyboard to the office. It was exactly as she remembered. This was Blake's space. This room and the workout room he'd built in the garage were his domain. He'd given her carte blanche with everything else, saying she should make the place feel like home to her because as long as she lived there, life couldn't get any better for him. She could paint the walls pink for all he cared. And she knew in the pit of her stomach she loved him back just as hard. How could they have gone from there to here in a few short years?

Chapter Eleven

"What are you working on?"

Blake blinked up at Alyssa. She stood there in his George Strait shirt and her old yoga pants, and his mind flashed to happier times when she'd show up in his office wearing only the shirt.

The corners of his lips upturned in a grin. He gave himself a mental slap because he didn't need to be going down that road where they ended up in a tangle in the sheets.

"I'm looking at routes to the doctor's office tomorrow. I took a look at those—" he motioned toward the divorce papers he'd retrieved from downstairs, which also grounded him in reality "—and found your address."

"Oh." She walked over beside him and her lilac and spring flower scent washed over him, stirring places he knew better than to allow. So, he distracted himself by focusing on the map instead of the long strands of hair clinging to the silky skin of her neck.

"This is your place." He pulled up the street view

of the bungalow on the northeastern outskirts of Houston. Then he stood up and offered her a seat.

She sat down and stared blankly as he grabbed a stool and pulled up beside her.

"May I?" She motioned toward the mouse.

"Be my guest."

She "walked" down the street and then "walked" back through a series of clicks on the road. And then recognition dawned as her eyes widened.

"My mom lives in an apartment a few blocks over. She and my dad lived there together, and she won't move. I tried to get her to live with me after he died, but she wasn't having it. Said she felt closer to him in their place despite me telling her she could move all her furniture in and replace mine if it made her more comfortable. She thought my dad hung the moon."

"So did you as I remember. The close relationship you had with your parents confirmed I was on the right track in wanting to ask you to marry me. I could never see myself falling for someone who didn't value family. We wouldn't agree in the long run." Not that he'd had much of a choice when he met her. He'd fallen fast and hard. They'd dated eighteen months to make sure the relationship wasn't too good to be true. Truth be told, he'd started thinking about a trip to the jeweler after their second date.

He'd had to slow his horses to give the relationship time to develop. He didn't need a year and a half to confirm what he already knew, but he thought he might scare her off by proposing on the second date.

When she didn't respond, he looked over at her. Lips compressed, gaze narrowed, she seemed to be concentrating like she was taking a math test.

"I don't quite remember it that way."

"That's strange." Had the blow to her head changed her thoughts in some way? Because he was one hundred percent certain she loved and admired her father.

"Something feels off. Like I loved my dad and thought he was great—"

"I wasn't exaggerating when I say you thought he hung the moon. He was your hero."

"What you're saying sounds familiar but way off in the distance."

"Could you and your father have had a fight that rubbed some of the shine off the way you saw him?"

"It's possible." The more she tried to focus, the more she looked like she was struggling to agree.

"Something must have happened. Trust me when I tell you the father-daughter bond was strong. Getting his approval to ask for your hand was probably the most stressful day of my life." He was only half-joking.

"Funny. What you're saying sounds familiar but when I think of my dad all I feel is tension. Like my mind is trying to send a warning and I can't quite grasp what it's trying to say. All I hear is *danger, danger.*"

Blake made a mental note of the shocking revelation. This was definitely out of character for the relationship he'd witnessed during their dating and married years. Something was out of whack. The fact that her father became ill and died could be the emotional block. His death had knocked the wind out of her.

There was a special bond between a father and daughter, he thought as he glanced at her belly.

Alyssa bit back a yawn. It was getting late and she had to be exhausted.

"Ready to call it a night?" he asked.

"That's probably a good idea. I can't remember the last time I was so tired. Or my back hurt this much. Or my legs literally felt like they could fall off. A bed sounds really good about now."

"You can take my bed. I'll sleep in the guest room."

"No." She shook her head. "I'm already putting you out enough. I'm not sleeping in your bed too."

"Well, it's softer than the one in the guest room and I figured you'd sleep better on it."

She was quiet for a long moment and something that looked a lot like fear darkened her eyes. Chin out, she seemed too stubborn to let it take hold. He remembered her reaction to him placing a blanket over her on the couch. She'd be too proud to ask for his help or admit she was scared to be alone.

"How about we make a deal?"

"I'm listening."

"The bed in the master is a king. We place a row

of pillows in the middle. You stick to your side and I'll stick to mine."

"Okay." There was no hesitation in her answer. He figured he hit the nail on the head about her being afraid.

Since he'd showered after his workout and hadn't done anything to make him work up a sweat since, he figured he could change into his boxers and grab a few hours of shut-eye. He wasn't kidding about it getting late. It was just after midnight. Life on a ranch started at 4:00 a.m., but he worked overnight. He would still be working his shift for a few more hours and climbing into bed as the sun was rising. The more he thought about returning to the ranch, the better he liked the idea.

Blake followed Alyssa into the bedroom as a bout of déjà vu struck. They'd walked this path more times than he cared to count under much better circumstances. He ducked into the bathroom and by the time he returned she was settled under the covers, hugging a pillow.

Even for someone his height and weight, a king bed would give enough space between them as long as they both stuck to their sides. Normally, Alyssa curled up around him, her head in the crook of his arm where she fit perfectly.

He didn't need to look at her swollen belly to realize how much that wouldn't work now. There were more arguments against falling into old patterns than types of ice cream. So, he climbed under the covers, turned off the light and muttered a good-night.

Minutes later, her steady, even breathing told him she was asleep. Part of him wanted to throw off the covers and get back to the computer to keep searching. The other part—the winning part—figured a few hours of sleep would help reset his mind for tomorrow. He needed to get his perspective back because the whole father-daughter bond comment had him wondering if his daughter would look up to him. Or would she wish someone else had fathered her?

Whoa. The pregnancy news was messing with his head.

If the child proved to be his, he would be there every step of the way. He would support her. And he would do whatever it took to have the kind of relationship that would make his father proud.

Blake knew he would never get too old to want to honor his father's memory.

THE ALARM BELL was faint but unmistakable. Blake shot up out of bed and snatched his phone from the nightstand. He retrieved his Colt 45 from the closet as he checked his cell.

Intruder.

On one of the cameras he'd set up while Alyssa had been in the shower last night, he saw a hooded figure move through the garage.

Intruder.

A second alarm sounded. There were at least two

people breeching the house. He checked the second camera that he'd set up at the front door. Blake moved to the closet and traded his Colt for a shotgun. He hit 911, thinking he was grateful to live so close to his substation. Buying this townhouse had been meant to shorten his commute. Now, he'd have officers here in five minutes.

"Alyssa, wake up. We have intruders."

She startled awake, sitting up and rubbing her eyes. Her sleepy look tugged at his heart.

"Dispatch, what's your emergency?"

"This is Officer Blake O'Connor. Two men are breaking into my townhouse. I need immediate assistance." He tossed the phone onto the bed and then helped Alyssa. Going downstairs was out of the question. The only option was to head up.

"Come on," he said quietly, looking into huge blue eyes. He needed to secure her in the attic so he could confront the intruders.

Alyssa gave a quick nod. He tucked the shotgun underneath his arm before clasping their hands. The doorway to the attic was in the hallway. He pulled the string, bringing down the ladder. He urged Alyssa to start climbing. She'd refused to go into the attic the entire time she'd lived in the townhouse. She'd fallen through a ceiling when she was six years old after following her father. He'd had no idea she was behind him. When he took a step back, she did too. Only there was no beam behind her, and she went all the way through, breaking her ankle on the landing. Ever since she'd been scared of a repeat.

This time, she climbed without looking back. He dashed into the bedroom to retrieve his cell. Still in his boxers, there was nowhere to stash it. He brought it to the base of the ladder, climbed up enough stairs to hand it to Alyssa. He checked the screen and saw a man in his kitchen and another in his living room.

Hells bells.

Blake stretched his hand up to give over the cell, but Alyssa clamped onto his wrist instead, tugging him up. His plan to surprise the men in the stairwell dissolved the minute he looked up and saw her expression. Sheet-white, he saw that she was trembling with fear.

Instead of folding the ladder and closing her in, he climbed the steps in silence. He brought the bottom half of the stairs with him and leveraged the string to bring up the door.

Because of Alyssa's fear, he'd put down wood flooring in the attic, figuring he'd surprise her when it was done. She was gone before he'd finished the job but that left only a two-by-two-foot spot in the corner.

Checking the phone, he saw one of the guys was already at the top of the stairs. The other waited at the bottom. The two were used to working together. They didn't need words, using hand signals to communicate their next steps.

The second intruder now joined the first on the

bedroom level, each going in a different direction to check rooms. Alyssa crouched low. Her chin jutted out in defiance. Her arms wrapped around her belly.

Blake studied his phone as intruder number one returned to the hallway. He glanced around and then looked up at the attic door. He seemed to be searching for the string. His face was covered in a hoodie and glasses. They weren't the shape of reading glasses or sunglasses for that matter. They looked like night-vision goggles. Not exactly military grade. These were smaller and most likely were bought online or at a spy shop. People could get almost anything on the internet these days.

"Pssst." Intruder number one called to his counterpart.

Blake settled the butt of his gun in the crook of his shoulder. He pointed the business end of the barrel at the door as he stood over it. Anyone who opened the door was going to be surprised. Since intruder number one didn't have a weapon in hand and Blake, as an officer, was responsible for every bullet he fired, he waited, barely daring to breathe.

He didn't so much as shift his weight because right now he had the advantage of surprise. As the second intruder joined the first, the distant wail of sirens pierced the air. The intruders froze. They locked on to each other and listened.

"Dammit," one of them said. Blake looked at Alyssa to see her reaction to the sound of the voice.

The look on her face told him everything he

needed to know. The men who, at the very least, were sitting on her at the trailer were inside his home.

The sirens pierced the air, getting closer. Blake held tight to the shotgun for a few more tense moments, the kind that raised blood pressure and made his heart pound against his ribs.

The sirens must've spooked them, because out of nowhere, they took off running toward the stairs. Both had weapons tucked in the waistband of their jeans. Good way to get their butts shot off.

It took every inch of resolve for Blake to stay put. He wouldn't risk giving away Alyssa's position or the fact she was staying with him. Though someone must have tipped them off. Either that, or they found him through investigating her.

"They're gone." Since he'd never hung up with Dispatch, he put the phone to his ear. "There were a pair of intruders inside my townhouse. They heard something…sirens maybe. Either way, they took off running. They're heading out my front door where I believe they have some type of vehicle waiting." He moved the phone from his mouth. "Wait here, okay?"

Alyssa nodded. She had a death grip on a wood beam.

He opened the door and descended the ladder, jumping when he reached the halfway-down point. He sprang into action, bolting toward the master bedroom to get the best view of the front of his home.

Just as he got to the window, a pair of squad cars

roared into the parking lot. The officers screeched to a stop, encircling the perps.

"That's them," he said into the phone to Dispatch.

Through the window, he heard one of the officers through a megaphone say, "Stop right there and put your hands where I can see 'em."

The perps looked at each other. A quick mental debate must've started and ended because when the third cruiser came squealing around the corner, they put their hands up in the air.

"They have weapons. Each has a gun tucked in the waistband of their jeans," he told Dispatch.

Through the speaker, he could hear her relaying the message.

"Keep those hands up high," one of the officers stated, his voice loud, authoritative, and high-pitched to gain attention and let the perps know he wasn't making a soft request. This was an order. It was a pitch only cops seemed to know.

One of the officers exited his vehicle, followed by a second. The third kept his weapon directed at the perps. "You on the left. Take two steps in the opposite direction of your friend here." The officer's door was open, and he was wedged in between the door and his vehicle as the pair of officers each took a perp. "On your knees. Keep your hands high."

The perps did. Each officer subdued one of the perps. Once the situation was secure, Blake returned to Alyssa to help her down the stairs. She climbed down.

"Did they get them?" Her face was still pale and sweat beaded on her forehead and upper lip.

"Yes."

"It was him. Gruff. I recognized his voice." She was trembling.

"Are you one hundred percent certain?"

"Yes. Absolutely."

With the guy in custody, maybe they'd finally get some answers.

Chapter Twelve

"Where are they now?" Alyssa's glance toward the master bedroom had Blake wondering if seeing the perps would be good for her stress levels. He was concerned for her. He was concerned about the baby. He'd basically developed a new ability to be concerned about everything that could possibly happen since learning his ex-wife was pregnant.

Blake linked their fingers and led her to the window, figuring she needed to see with her own eyes the men responsible for making her life a living hell recently were headed behind bars. In the dark, the perps wouldn't be able to see them, and yet she still backed away from the window once she saw the scene unfolding in the parking lot.

"I recognized the voice." She studied them. "They basically look like how I pictured them in my mind. I thought Gruff would be stocky and probably look almost as pregnant as I am. Nasal, to me, was going to be the tall, skinny one. This guy isn't quite as tall as I imagined but he's skinny."

The two were, in fact, as she'd described them. He had other problems on his hands. His front door had been broken into. There was no way he wanted to leave his home and personal items unprotected and he figured he'd get about as much sleep as a bear in summer at this point.

"How did you know they were here? I don't re-member having cameras set up when we lived to-gether?" she asked.

"I spent the better half of my teenage years tracking poachers when I wasn't in school or rid-ing fences." Most people didn't realize how much of cattle ranching was keeping the herd safe on the property. Fences kept strays from wandering and needed repair on a near-constant basis considering the sheer amount of land his family owned. They owned mineral rights too, and that was where the real family fortune resided. "To make a long story short, I set up cameras at the two main entrances of the house while you were in the shower earlier and the alarm on my phone alerted me."

Since his front door was open, he needed to get downstairs before the neighbors started wandering in. Hell, the neighbors, stray dogs or anything else the wind might blow in.

Linking their fingers again, he led her downstairs.

"How are you? Everything okay?" He glanced at her stomach and saw the T-shirt move. "What just happened there?"

"She kicked. I swear this kid is either going to be

a swimmer or a black belt in kung fu." She grimaced and the shirt moved again. "See."

"Crazy to think there's a kid in there."

"Do you want to feel her move?"

He should say a resounding no. Maybe it was the father-daughter bond he'd been thinking about earlier. His own father barely had a chance to get to know his only daughter before she was taken away from him.

"Yes. I do." This wouldn't change anything between him and Alyssa. She'd made her choice and he'd learned to live with it. The kid, however, was innocent. She shouldn't suffer because her parents weren't getting along.

Alyssa took his hand and placed it on her belly where the kicks had been. She lowered her voice and said, "Hey, little bean, this is your father."

Nothing happened.

"Just hold on a minute," Alyssa said. "Once she gets going, she never stops this soon."

He waited.

Still nothing. Maybe the kid didn't like him already. Or he was too unfamiliar. "How far along did you say you are?"

"Eight months," she said.

Meaning he had a few weeks to get ready.

"Can I ask a question?"

He nodded, removing his hand from her belly. The shirt moved the second he stopped touching Alyssa.

"Why didn't you ask the doctor for a paternity

test? It would have been easy enough. I think it's literally as simple as a spit swab."

"If you say I'm the father, I don't doubt your word." He shrugged his shoulder. Part of him had tried to put up the argument that he couldn't be the child's father. Simple math said he probably was, as long as there was no one else in the picture. "If you want the test, we can get it."

"I may not remember everything that happened in recent months, but I'm clear on who her father is. There could only be one option. I'm sure I didn't leave you for someone else. I haven't been with anyone else. I wouldn't want to be with anyone else."

He let the last sentence slide. It was his bruised ego that wanted it to be true. Time to change the subject.

"Do you want to put your feet up while I check the entrances?" He motioned toward the couch.

"I'm wide awake now, so, yes." She moved over to the couch and then stacked a few pillows to prop up her back. She lay across it lengthwise.

He addressed the front door first. It had been left slightly ajar, so he opened it—careful not to interfere with any prints—and then tested the locking mechanism. Professional job. The perp used a universal key. The good news was the lock wasn't broken. The bad news was that it clearly needed a dead bolt added.

An officer met him at the door.

"Evening, sir," the officer started. "Are you Blake O'Connor?"

"Yes, sir." Blake checked the man's name tag. It was a big department and he didn't recognize this officer. "Thank you for stopping by, Officer Barton."

"May I come inside, Officer O'Connor?"

"Yes, sir. And, please, call me Blake." He was careful to open the door fully. "The perps entered through the front door and the back. You'll probably want to dust the knobs. Although, I'm almost certain they had on some type of gloves."

"Yes, sir. They did."

Well, that explained why the officer hadn't brought his dusting kit to the door with him. He knew he didn't need it.

Blake introduced the officer to Alyssa. Barton took her statement, and then Blake's. By the time he finished, a knock at the door interrupted them.

He opened it to find Liz standing there. All five feet two inches of fury. She stalked past before barking a few orders at Barton. Apparently, the two knew each other fairly well. He excused himself after she told him to go file the report.

Once he was gone, she turned to Blake. "Tell me what the hell happened here tonight."

Blake went over the story again for her. "I need to get someone out to dead bolt this door and the one in the garage."

Liz glanced over at Alyssa who had closed her eyes and turned onto her side.

"She's bringing trouble to your doorstep, Blake," Liz said low and under her breath.

Alyssa blinked her eyes open. She seemed to think better of making a comment.

"That's out of line, Liz. Everything that happens to her while she's carrying my child is my business." He kept his voice low as he motioned for Liz to follow him into the next room.

"The kid is yours?" Liz didn't bother to hide her shock, or her disdain. More of that anger was rolling off her. He knew she cared about him, but this was over-the-top.

"The timeline of her pregnancy matches up to our relationship." Although, he didn't think sexual relations with his then-wife were anyone else's business.

"Please tell me you got a paternity test."

ALYSSA WASN'T SURE how long she'd nodded off. Lack of quality sleep combined with late-term pregnancy had her dozing off every chance she got. The sun was rising, and the house was quiet. She pushed up to sitting to find Blake at the table with his laptop, nursing a cup of coffee.

"Is there any chance you have decaf?"

"No. Sorry."

"I figured as much."

"Never saw the point." He smiled and a dozen butterflies released in her chest.

"Neither did I until I got pregnant."

"Yeah, I see your point. I hadn't thought about the sacrifices you've been making. Has it been awful?"

"Sometimes." She figured he wouldn't judge her for being honest. "Once I got over the initial shock and sacrifices, it got a lot easier. Then she started moving around in there and I guess I was hooked. Suddenly, it was easy to forget how hard it was at first. It helped that I stopped throwing up every five minutes."

He made a face.

"It wasn't that bad in retrospect. At the time, I was probably pretty dramatic about it, though." She laughed as she looked around. "The door?"

"Had a locksmith change out the lock and add a dead bolt."

"And I didn't hear it?"

"You were pretty out of it."

"How out of it do you have to be not to hear a hammer?"

"It was an electric screwdriver and my guy was stealth." He picked up his mug. "Are you hungry?"

"Is that a real question?" Now, she really laughed. "I'm always hungry now. Even when I don't think I'm hungry, I've found that I can eat."

She joined him in the kitchen.

"Pregnancy agrees with you." He looked at her with appreciation and it was the first time in months someone looked at her with anything but a sweet smile or a look of apology. She figured the reactions to her pregnancy from strangers must mirror whatever their experience was. The sweet ones must've had an easy time of it. The others, well, maybe not so much. Either way, she always smiled back.

Blake had always made a mean omelet. This morning was no exception. She literally groaned with pleasure while she ate it. He added fresh greens and a sliced tomato. Pure food heaven.

"Have the police called?"

"Gruff's real name is Christopher Desmond. And the one you called Nasal is Jordan Bennett. Do either of those names ring a bell?" He picked up the plate after she'd cleaned it.

Nothing automatically came to mind. She tried to reach deep and came up with nothing. "No idea who they are."

"Liz called your office to ask to speak to one and then the other. Neither one works for you or worked for your father. She had the manager check the HR files." He paused. "Doesn't mean they aren't connected to the business in some way. The manager didn't recognize the names and they don't work at Hazel Imports. That's as much as we know for now."

"At least they're locked up and we know who they are." There was some relief in knowing these guys were off the streets. "I forgot to tell you last night that my mom checked in with me. I saw it on your phone. She made it safely to her friend's house."

"She might want to stay there a couple of days to be on the safe side." Blake's cell buzzed. He checked the screen. "It's Liz."

After hearing Liz's comments last night, Alyssa couldn't say she was thrilled. This seemed like a good time to remind herself they could use all the help they could get. As the saying went, she wouldn't look a gift horse in the mouth.

Taking in a deep breath, she moved into the kitchen and refilled her water glass. While she was there, she figured she'd make herself useful and rinse off the breakfast dishes. A mild cramp was followed by a stronger one as she bent over to load the bottom rack of the dishwasher. She glanced at the clock. Her doctor's appointment was still a ways off. She could make it until then unless the cramps started coming more regularly or hit as hard as the ones last night. Stress? Dehydration?

"Okay, thanks for the information." Blake paused. "Yes. She's awake." He was silent for a few beats. "All right. Talk to you later."

Blake ended the call and joined her in the kitchen. He took one look at her and asked, "Everything okay?"

"Yes. All good here." She forced a smile.

He stopped and stared at her for a long moment. "You sure?"

"Yes." She did a thumbs-up move that was as cheesy as it felt. "What did Liz say?"

"The perps are asking for a deal in exchange for information about who is truly behind all this."

"That's a good thing, right?" She didn't use her thumb to help communicate this time.

"If the information turns out to be solid, it will be."

"Are the chances pretty good we'll get what we need from them?" She wasn't sure how she felt about this being a bigger operation. Or about how many other women might have been locked inside that same closet. That same bedroom. The flooring had been ripped up. Had someone been inside there for days? Weeks? Chipping away at the flooring, praying to open it enough to make a breakaway? The thought sent a cold chill down her back.

"I want the names of Bus Stop and the Judge. That's what they're promising."

"You don't think the Judge is an actual judge, do you?" It wouldn't surprise her, but it would mean they were up against someone on the inside of the legal system. That was almost unthinkable.

"I hope not. I'd like to think everyone who takes the same pledge I did means it just as much. Criminals are scum, but a person sworn to protect who turns is lethal."

"I believe the same thing." She was nodding as he spoke.

"It would also make the case a lot more complicated, so I'm hoping it has a different meaning."

She hadn't thought about it in those terms, but he made a good point. *Complicated* and *dangerous* were two terms she didn't want assigned to her case.

"How long will it take to make the deal and find out?"

"A few hours. Maybe. Hopefully sooner. There's

usually a bit of negotiating involved, so it can take time to reach an agreement on both sides."

"What do we do in the meantime?" Every minute counted while her life hung in the balance. Alyssa wasn't as worried for herself as she was for the baby.

"Keep a low profile."

"If those two found us their bosses must know where we are," she pointed out.

"Which is why I wondered if you'd want to go to the ranch to stay for a few days until all this blows over."

"Are you serious?" The last place she wanted to show up pregnant after a divorce was his family's ranch. They were good people, but *uncomfortable* didn't begin to describe how she would feel surrounded by O'Connors under the circumstances. She'd walked away from the family that had taken her in and treated her like one of their own. They'd accepted her with open arms and hearts, and she'd repaid their kindness by divorcing Blake. It just didn't add up.

"Yes." He softened his eyes and cocked his head to one side. "No matter what is going on between us, the baby is my first priority right now. I can't think of a better place to keep her safe."

"Poachers make it onto the land. Your father was killed there." She wished she could reel those words back in the minute she heard them come out of her mouth. She'd had a knee-jerk reaction and wanted more than anything to take it back. She put her hands up, palms out, hoping to stop him long enough to apologize. "I didn't mean to say—"

Rather than get angry with her, he stood there. A look of understanding was stamped on his features. His hands were at his sides, open, with his palms facing her. "I know it's asking a lot."

She issued a sharp sigh. It would have almost been easier if he'd gotten mad at her. She didn't want to suffer the embarrassment of showing up in her present condition without remembering the past eight months of her life without Blake. And yet, he was right. This was her daughter's family. Considering it was only Alyssa and her mother on the Hazel side, the baby could use all the family she could get. And Alyssa was going to have to face the O'Connors at some point.

She folded her arms across her chest, resting them on her burgeoning belly, considering her options. "The ranch is pretty far from here. It'll be impossible to check in at work let alone my apartment and with my doctor."

"It's time to leave the investigation up to my colleagues. If these jerks are part of a bigger organization, it could get messier. In fact, I'd like to pick up your mother and keep her at the ranch too. What do you think about putting her up in the guest room at the main house? I'm certain my mother would love the company and it would give her something to focus on besides losing my father."

The way he was talking, the men behind bars

seemed like the least of her problems. And that sent an icy chill racing down her back.

"When did you think would be a good time to head that way? If I agree?" She was short on options.

"After the doctor's appointment."

"Speaking of which, what if I actually do go into labor, Blake? What if I'm too far away from my doctor and the hospital? The ranch is remote." She was starting to freak out a little bit when she thought through the possible issues with the plan.

"You're eight months along, right?"

She nodded.

"Which should mean you have at the very least a few more weeks before it's 'go' time. Right?" His voice was a study in calm.

She nodded again. He was being rational whereas she was working off raw emotion—emotion that was heightened thanks to pregnancy hormones and the fact that some random scary people were after her.

"Then we should be fine for a few days until my fellow law enforcement officers can get a handle on who is behind this." He walked over and closed the dishwasher before taking her hand and walking her over to the kitchen table.

All kinds of warning bells sounded at the underlying message. She was potentially in even more danger than before, now that two perps had been arrested.

Chapter Thirteen

"I'll do it."

Blake wasn't quite ready to let his guard down after hearing those three words. They were a step in the right direction.

"Thank you for your trust," he responded. She needed to know her confidence meant something to him.

"If it can help keep her safe, I'd walk through fire at this point." Alyssa's hands went to her belly. He noticed she did that whenever she was stressed. She'd cradle her bump or rub her belly like she was trying to soothe the baby. Her voice was different now too. She had a calming quality when she spoke. He didn't think she was aware of what she was doing so much as acting on instinct. She was going to make a great mother.

Shared birthdays and every other Christmas wasn't how he imagined his family would look. Alyssa was as much his family as the baby. He would do whatever he could to ease her burden now that he was in on the pregnancy. His only regret was that he didn't know about it sooner. He couldn't imagine going through this alone.

Alyssa had her mother, even though their roles seemed reversed to him in the last year or so of the marriage.

"Believe it or not, we're making progress."

"I'm still in shock those jerks would break into a police officer's home. I thought we'd be safe here."

"You are. Both of you. For now. I don't want to tempt fate and it's obvious these perps know where I live. They figured out you came here, so we have to get on the move, but we have to be smart about it. Give the legal system time to do its job." He believed in the institution despite the fact it had let his family down.

"You're right. I feel like I put you in danger by coming here." She stared up at him with those wide eyes. He'd been thinking about the kiss they'd shared more than he should allow himself to. Being this close wasn't helping control the urge to touch her. He brought his hand up, brushing the backs of his fingers against her cheek. Her skin was just as silky as he remembered. Those eyes were just as beautiful as he remembered. And her lips were just as pink as he remembered. Before he could stop himself, he dipped his head and brushed a kiss against her mouth. At least he had enough sense to stop there.

He leaned his forehead against hers and did his level best to slow his racing pulse.

"I'm glad you showed up here, Alyssa. You did the right thing." His defenses lowered for just a few moments even as he reminded himself not to get too comfortable.

"I just realized something. I've had a strange feeling that in some way leaving you would protect you. Did I know these people were after me? Did I do something illegal? Immoral?"

"You couldn't have. That isn't who you are." He was adamant on that point. She would never willingly or knowingly do something illegal or immoral.

"What if I did, though?"

He shook his head. There was not a shadow of a doubt in his mind she wasn't a hardened criminal or someone who took advantage of other people. If she'd wanted money all she had to do was ask for it in the divorce. He believed in love and spending his life with someone, so he hadn't asked her to sign a prenup. He wouldn't go into a marriage planning for its failure. Did marriages fail? Of course, they did. His was proof. He just couldn't go into any union thinking it might end. He took his vows seriously and believed he was marrying the right one.

"I just have this strong sense that I left you in order to protect you," she said.

"From what?" Could that explain her actions? Wrap up his heartbreak in a neat little box?

"Me." She blinked up at him. Her eyes were glittery with something that looked a whole lot like need. A shot straight to his heart fueled his desire to kiss her again. Maintaining distance was key to keeping his feelings in check—feelings that were on a mission of their own since finding out he was going to become a father. It was natural to be attracted to the child's mother, but was it stupid to act on it?

Stupidity be damned, he went for it. Like gravity, keeping his feet planted firmly on the earth, his heart was pulled toward her.

The kiss was tender at first. He took his time running his tongue across her bottom lip before dipping the tip inside her sweet lips. His heart took another hit when she moaned against his mouth.

His breath quickened and his heart raced as they deepened the kiss. They'd gone from zero to sixty in a matter of seconds. He needed to cool his jets or risk letting this get out of control.

A large part of him wanted to run with it if he was being honest. See where it might end up. *End* being the word that told him to slow down. As much as he wanted—*needed?*—to believe she'd left him for altruistic reasons, the simple fact was she should have talked to him about it first. Making the decision for him, not giving him a say in their relationship, doused the flame gaining ground inside him.

He brought his hands up to cup her face, ending the kiss. She opened her eyes slowly, those blue irises contrasting against the white.

This seemed like a good time to remind himself just how heartbroken he'd been. His ego had taken a monumental hit and he'd licked his wounds, when no one was around to take notice. His life had crumbled despite the show he put on meant to make others think he had it together. Liz hadn't been fooled. But then she probably knew him better than most. It was a fact he was beginning to realize sat like sour milk for Alyssa.

"MIND IF I go through my boxes upstairs while we wait for my doctor's appointment?" Alyssa asked, needing to put some space between her and Blake so she could straighten out her thoughts. She'd wanted to kiss Blake as much as he wanted to kiss her. A mistake? Maybe, but she was tired of sitting on the sidelines and not going after what she wanted.

Of course, the pregnancy complicated matters tenfold. The baby had to come first. Period. That was a no-brainer.

"Go for it." Blake studied her as she walked past him.

She had hours to kill before her appointment and being anywhere in his vicinity clogged her thinking. The attraction that was the strongest she'd ever experienced was still on full tilt. He was smart, had a sense of humor that fit hers and had a certain undeniable charm. On top of those qualities, he was one of the, if not *the*, hottest men she'd ever laid eyes on. The description *rock-hard* was created for a body like his. Underneath that big brain and quick wit was the kind of person who would put himself in harm's way to help someone he cared about.

Climbing the stairs knocked the wind out of her. She stood at the top, and a shiver raced down her spine when she glanced at the ladder that was still down. Facing her source of fear, she walked over, closed up the ladder and sent it toward heaven. Enough of that.

The blinds to the guest room were open and the place was bathed in sunlight. She walked to the closet and opened the door. A box was open. This one must be where her yoga pants, and present source of comfort, came from. It struck her that she'd been in such a hurry to leave that she took off without a few of her all-time favorite items.

Alyssa pulled the box toward the bed and plopped down on her backside. Sifting through the clothes, she realized just how much she'd left behind. A favorite sweater. Her all-time favorite hoodie. Leggings that were her go-to bottoms. Strange.

Had she believed she would be coming back?

Divorce papers were a sure sign she had no intention of trying to make her marriage work—a marriage to a man she loved and also had a deep-seeded need to protect from…what? Nasal and Gruff? Bus Stop or the Judge?

The first pair were clearly henchmen. The others? She especially didn't like the name of the second one. There were implications there she hoped wasn't the case. If someone from law enforcement was somehow involved, it was over. There'd be no going back. She might as well change her name and

leave the country. Bring up her baby on a remote island or over in the Eastern Bloc. Somewhere people
went to disappear.

So, yeah, there were a lot of holes in the plan.
Not the least of which was the fact that Blake would
never stand for his child to be brought up in a place
where he couldn't be part of her life. Then, there was
his family to consider. The O'Connors were tight-
knit. They were a family rooted deep in the fabric
of Texas ranching. Alyssa couldn't ignore the fact it
would be difficult to hide an O'Connor child. Was
that the real reason she'd taken off without telling
Blake about the pregnancy?

Did she have the order of events wrong in her
mind? It was highly possible she'd found out about
the pregnancy and the discovery fueled her hurried
escape. There was also the timing of her father's
death to consider.

Alyssa believed she and Blake had the kind of
relationship where they talked. Late into the night,
in fact, after a round of the best sex of her life. And,
yes, she remembered that detail very clearly. The kiss
in the kitchen helped bring back a flood of memories of just how heated their passion had been and
how connected she'd felt to her husband in every
way possible.

Right now, she would stick with the divorce happening first and the pregnancy news after. So, what
would make her leave? Why would men be after

her? And how could any of this be tied to her father's death?

His cause of death was certain: pneumonia. Not exactly a reason for scary men to come out of the woodwork to chase her. The family business wasn't one that made her father, or her for that matter, wealthy. It gave them a decent life. Plenty of food. Her dad hadn't driven a showy car or displayed any signs that he was involved in anything illegal. As far as she knew, he never missed a tax deadline or payment.

According to Blake, her father's death had sent her into a downward spiral. She could easily see how that might happen as close as she was to the man. Losing him would be one of the most difficult things to overcome.

The part that made no sense was her pushing away the only man she ever loved. And she had loved her husband. He'd never objected to having a baby. To be fair, they'd talked about having kids someday *way* down the road. Like years later once they were ready. A change in plans with a surprise pregnancy might have been a game changer for their plans but it never would have been a deal breaker.

She snapped back to the fact her husband, *ex*-husband, would have been there for her no matter what. That's just how Blake was made. He had more honor in his little finger than most had in their whole bodies.

The sound of feet shuffling up the stairs turned

her attention toward the door. For a split-second, her heart leaped in her throat and her hand came up to cover a gasp. The second she saw Blake's silhouette from down the hall, she exhaled a slow breath.

Once she saw the look on his face, her pulse pounded.

"Liz just called. There was a glitch in the paperwork. Christopher Desmond and Jordan Bennett were released."

"What? How?"

"Your guess is as good as mine." He shrugged before glancing at the box. "Is there anything in there you can use?"

"We need to get out of here, don't we?"

"Yes, but I doubt they'd be stupid enough to come back here. They have to know cops are watching the place. Liz requested a squad car in the front and back of the house while we gather our things. She sent them over before giving me a call because she didn't want to risk them not getting here in time."

This wasn't the time to be jealous, but Liz sure did her best to attend to Blake's needs before he even realized he needed something. Of course, the woman was looking out for her former partner. Some of her comments this morning crossed a line. But Alyssa couldn't be picky about who helped them at the moment. She wasn't in a position to complain or turn down assistance no matter how much she wanted to give Liz a piece of her mind. The officer had made it clear she wasn't helping Alyssa.

"I'm not sure much of this will fit anymore. I wish I could swing by my apartment to pick up a few things." She was also hoping seeing the place again would jog her memory. The sensation that everything she needed to know was just out of reach frustrated her to no end.

"It can probably be arranged. After the doctor's appointment."

"Where will we go in the meantime?"

He walked inside and sat on the edge of the bed. "That's a good question. We can wait it out at the station."

"Yours?" She didn't want to ask if Liz would be there. She had a haunting suspicion, though.

"Yes."

"If the guys figured out your address, won't they also realize where you work?" It was a lame excuse.

"We can stay right here until your appointment."

"What if different guys show up this time? Bus Stop or the Judge? They could walk right past the uniformed officers and no one would know we're in danger." She might be reaching here but it seemed possible.

"They've been told to allow no one past."

"Okay." The news made her feel a little bit better despite the walls closing in around her. "I found this in the box." She picked up their wedding album.

He stared out the window before getting up and closing the blinds. It was a stark reminder of the danger they were still in. The idea this situation could get worse caused her stress levels to skyrocket.

Not good for the baby. Granted, this situation was…extreme. There was no questioning the fact. But she didn't want her baby feeling all the anxiety coursing through her right now. Deep breaths weren't helping but focusing on her wedding day brought her panic levels down a few notches.

"Mind if I take a look?" she asked.

"Suit yourself."

"Do we have time?" Giving herself something to focus on besides the danger that could be lurking outside might calm her down.

"Yes."

She flipped through the pages. The happy looks on everyone's faces, including hers, made her smile. "I remember this like it was yesterday. Three years went by in a flash."

"Only two of those were married. This last one has been going through the divorce," he pointed out. She'd clearly struck a nerve with the photos. And yet, she wanted to remember them in happier times.

"I remember this being the second happiest day of my life."

He quirked a brow. "Second?"

"Yep. The first was the day you asked me to be your wife." She remembered it like it was yesterday. He'd taken her to the ranch for a family dinner like he did sometimes on Sundays. The house was full of people, laughter and good conversation. Nothing out of the ordinary except this time her parents had been invited. Blake had done it once before and she'd been suspicious then. This time, she was completely caught off guard. She liked that he was including her parents. They rarely ever went out. The two of them sat in front of the TV every night eating dinner off TV trays. Their relationship was mutual quiet companionship.

It was the exact opposite of what Alyssa shared with Blake. Theirs was built on fire, passion and a bond so tight she thought on her wedding day it could never be broken.

Blake leaned over to her, shoulder to shoulder, and said, "The kiss we shared downstairs. It can't happen again."

"I know." There was no enthusiasm in her response despite him hitting the nail on the head.

Had she been so far off base, so wrong, that it couldn't be repaired now?

A relationship was built on one key element that would be missing from here on out…trust.

Chapter Fourteen

Blake checked the time. The appointment was getting closer. They could probably swing by early and maybe badge their way inside. Doctors were always generous to police officers and vice versa. No cop he knew wanted to show up in an ER in a bad way and have the doctor hesitate because he recognized a jerk who gave him a speeding ticket for going a couple miles over the speed limit.

The relationship was reciprocal. Maybe he could use some of that goodwill to bump up Alyssa's appointment and get them on the road a little earlier. Despite the few naps she'd had and the couple hours of sleep she'd gotten last night, she looked tired. The cramps she'd experienced earlier had him concerned. He was still on sea legs when it came to knowing what to do to help her. He needed a crash course in pregnancy and kids. He figured he could learn all he needed to know on the ranch between his mother and brothers.

So far, based on the fact he'd kissed his pregnant

ex a couple of times—kisses that sent his pulse racing just thinking about them—and that he was barely keeping her out of the clutches of men determined to hurt her, he'd say he wasn't crushing it.

Alyssa closed the wedding album and tucked it inside the box. She did so with such care that his traitorous heart clenched. So much had happened in the past twenty-four hours, he was just beginning to process everything. Normally, he needed to get still for a few minutes at some point every day to let his mind do the work so he could relax. This situation was coming at him and through him like a runaway train, and there was no time to process. Pregnancy. Fatherhood. Those weren't the terms that immediately came to mind when he thought about their relationship. Hell, he'd never expected to see Alyssa again since she'd refused to even talk to him except through lawyers after she left.

He should have a whole lot to say to her about the way she'd left things except that enough time had passed for him to let go of all the pent-up anger he'd felt. Time was the great healer. And even if he didn't exactly feel healed, he'd accepted her decision. Hearing she made a difficult choice in order to protect him was a gut punch. Protect him from what? Or should he say whom?

The truth of the matter was that she hadn't trusted him enough to tell him what was going on. Did she think he wouldn't listen to her or take her seriously? Did she think he would laugh at her?

Yes, there were jerks after her, but he was a cop. He had resources.

"I think this pair of yoga pants might work. I've put on a lot of weight with the pregnancy." Her cheeks flushed with embarrassment.

He put his hand on her arm, ignoring all the electricity pinging between them at the contact. "You're even more beautiful now, if that's at all possible."

His comment was rewarded with a smile warm enough to light a dozen little campfires in his chest. And, yes, put him at risk of leaning over to close the distance between them and press another kiss to those pink lips of hers.

Bad idea.

So, he distracted himself with his phone, checking his email while she went through the last of the items in the box.

"There are a couple of things in here that might still fit. Basically, underwear at this point." She held up a pair. Pink. Silk. And he suddenly got an image he didn't need running around in his thoughts. Although pink was now his favorite color and he couldn't get the image of the last time she'd worn them out of his thoughts.

Blake pushed off the bed and strode into the master bedroom. He grabbed his weekend hunting duffel from the closet, figuring it never hurt to be prepared. He was good at being a cop in part because he was paranoid. The paranoia made him consider every possible scenario when walking into a dangerous

situation. It made him more aware of his surround-
ings and everything that could go wrong. It had saved
his life on more than one occasion.

"If we could somehow pick up my laptop, I would
be able to dig into work files and see if this mess is
somehow related to the company." Alyssa stood at
the bedroom door. He'd heard her walking down
the hallway.

"We can swing by your apartment after the doctor visit. Make sure your mom is ready because we'll
pick her up before heading to the ranch." He fished
his cell out of his pocket and walked it over to her.

As he handed it over, it buzzed. Liz's name came
up and he could swear Alyssa's muscles tensed up.
Did she have a problem with his former partner? For
someone who was supposed to be so observant, he'd
missed the fact his wife didn't like his partner. Of
course, when it came to Alyssa, he seemed to have
a real blind spot.

He put the call on speaker.

"Hey, Liz. I'm here with Alyssa and you're on
speaker. Is that okay with you?"

"Yeah, sure." Her hesitation had him realizing the
feeling between the two was mutual. How had he
missed it? He'd known Liz wasn't Alyssa's favorite
person, but this was bigger. Based on Liz's reaction
and a few of the things she'd said about his ex, he
saw this went both ways.

"What's up?" The faster she got to the point, the
better.

"I was calling to let you know the two men we had in custody were found in a parked car on the side of the road shot execution style."

"Any idea who the car belonged to?"

"Yes, Christopher Desmond." Her voice was all business and a little colder than usual. Was having Alyssa on the call throwing Liz for a loop?

"His own car picked him up and then he was shot in it?" Blake asked, a little surprised it had gone down like that. Someone had to be driving Desmond's vehicle.

"That about sums it up."

Alyssa brought her hand up to cover her mouth. She moved over to the bed and sat down, a shocked look on her face.

"Who filled out the paper that let them out of jail in the first place?" Little had they known they would be safer locked up. Obviously, someone couldn't risk them talking. The Judge? Was he connected to law enforcement in some way?

"A rookie."

"Are you telling me this was a mistake?" Blake couldn't hide his frustration. He smacked his palm against the table.

"Collins said he got a phone call stating the two needed to be released immediately. He was told paperwork was coming down the pike but that their attorney was on his way."

"And he released them on someone's word?"

Rookie or not, the man needed to be fired if that was the case.

"No. He checked the database and got the okay to release them. He walked them to the door and set them free."

"Inside job?" His gaze moved to Alyssa, who'd gone sheet white.

"Naturally, I want to say no. I don't think I'd have a leg to stand on if I did, though. As much as I hate to admit it, this could be coming from the inside."

"The Judge?"

"YOUR GUESS IS as good as mine."

Alyssa's heart sank when she heard Liz's words. None of this sounded good. Not at all what Alyssa wanted to hear. Based on Blake's expression, thin lips and narrowed gaze, he was on the same page.

"Detectives are on their way to process the scene," Liz continued.

"Keep me posted if they find anything." Blake issued a sharp sigh.

"You know I will." Liz ended the call without addressing Alyssa, which got under her skin. She knew she shouldn't let the woman bother her but there was something about her attachment to Blake that didn't sit right.

Again, Liz was helping with the investigation, so Alyssa should keep quiet about her concerns over the woman's constant contact with Blake.

"Are you ready to roll?" Blake asked.

"Yes." She needed to get out of there. The walls felt like they were closing in since hearing the news about the murders and she needed air. Suddenly, the thought of going to the ranch to breathe in fresh, country air wasn't so awful. She wanted to disappear in a place where she and the baby could be safe until the birth if she were honest.

She had the family business to think about. How would she keep up financial support for her mother if it failed? How long could she be away before trouble started? Before the small operation started cracking?

Best as she could remember, she wasn't planning on taking a whole lot of time off for maternity leave. That was the thing about running a small business. She'd learned she could pick her own hours, but she still had to work all of them anyway.

Pushing up to standing, she found that one of her legs had fallen asleep and she went back down. Thankfully, she landed on the bed on her backside. Other than embarrassing, there was no real harm done. Based on the concerned look on Blake's face, she wasn't as graceful as she'd hoped.

"Are you all right?" He was standing next to her in a matter of seconds.

"Fine. I'm good." As long as embarrassment couldn't kill her, she'd be okay.

He held out his forearm and she took it, using it as leverage to pull herself up.

"See. I did it."

"You're sure?" His gaze traveled over her.

"One hundred percent." She threw her arms up to show him she could balance without holding on. "I'm so good."

He nodded before picking up the duffel he'd set out. He placed it on the bed and unzipped it. "Want to put your things in here?"

She gathered up the few pairs of underwear and placed them inside. He immediately zipped it up and she saw he had an extra weapon inside. He went to the closet and took his holster out. He put it on along with a Houston PD windbreaker. Next, he secured his service weapon in the holster.

Duffel in one hand, he took her hand in his and then linked their fingers. She couldn't help but notice how well they fit together. And how comforted she felt every time they had a physical connection. When this was over, leaving him again was going to hurt.

She glanced down at her belly and almost laughed out loud. It was ironic more than funny. She and Blake would be connected in some fashion for the rest of their lives by the little bean.

Speaking of laughing, pretty much nothing was funny except that if she didn't laugh a little bit she would probably go out of her mind from the stress. She had to take mental breaks, or she'd overthink the situation and that wouldn't be good for her or the baby.

Besides, she was more determined now than ever to figure out who Bus Stop and the Judge were. She would turn over every stone if she had to in order to find out why Nasal and Gruff were murdered and who pulled strings to have them released from jail so they could be shot.

An icy chill raced down her spine at the thought these ruthless men were after her and would do anything to stop her. What information could she possibly have? She and her dad ran a small business. They weren't sitting on a fortune. Norman Hazel was the most normal person in the world. He'd shown up to her soccer games when she was a kid. He'd threatened never to let her date and then had a "talk" with her prom date before she could walk outside the front door. As far as she knew, he stayed inside the law.

Blake helped her climb inside his Jeep that was parked inside the garage. He fired off a text and she imagined he was letting Liz know the two of them were on the move. Liz. What was it about his former partner that had Alyssa's stomach twisted up in a knot? Blake wasn't interested in the woman. He looked at her like any other coworker.

Alyssa wasn't sexist, so it wasn't the fact that Liz was a woman in police work that bothered her. Chalking it up to missing her ex, Alyssa set those thoughts aside. She would have her laptop soon, and she could start digging around there for answers. It was as good a place as any.

Blake tucked the duffel in the back seat before claiming the driver's side.

"I forgot to let my mom know we'd be coming

for her. Mind if I use your phone to send a text?" she asked.

"No. Go right ahead." He handed it over and then hit the garage door opener.

She sent a short message, letting her mom know she'd be by to pick her up shortly. Her mother didn't respond right away. She rarely ever kept her phone with her, and it seemed like half the time she had the volume off so she could "hear" her shows better. And then there were the times her mother just left the phone in another room and didn't think about it.

Alyssa's phone was practically glued to her hand at all times. She missed it and felt oddly disconnected from the world without it. For a minute at the townhouse, it had been nice to escape reality. But now she wished she had her phone with her. And while she was wishing, she might as well request her purse. Not having ID, a credit card or cash made her feel oddly naked as well.

The ride to her doctor's office was quiet. Not awkward. Just silent companionship. She missed that about Blake. They could be right next to each other, one reading while the other surfed the web, and neither had to fill the air with words. Just being around him gave her a settled feeling she'd never experienced with anyone else. There was an excitement too. Butterflies in the stomach and her heart catching in her throat when he looked at her. The feeling never stopped, not even after the wedding. She remembered feeling like the luckiest person in the world that day.

Her parents had given her a solid upbringing. She was admittedly closer to her dad than her mother, loved by both. She'd always wanted siblings, but none came. Her mom had been around but distant. It wasn't until years later that she'd learned her mother had been pregnant as a teen, and forced to give her child up for adoption, a daughter.

Alyssa chalked up the emotional distance between her and her mother to the loss. Hand to belly, Alyssa couldn't fathom giving up her child. But then, she wasn't sixteen and under her parents' thumb. Her grandparents were the stern, old-fashioned types. Religious to a fault.

She couldn't imagine the looks on their faces when their only daughter came home pregnant as a teenager. Mother met Alyssa's dad while volunteering part-time at an animal shelter. He went in for a puppy and came out with the best thing that ever happened to him, according to him. They loved each other and, in some ways, Alyssa felt like the odd man out.

Meeting Margaret O'Connor had made Alyssa understand her own mother better. Mrs. O'Connor had her child stolen from her crib, in her own home. Every parent's worst nightmare played out in her life. And yet, the loss caused her to be closer to her boys in some ways. She'd picked herself up and moved on with life because of them, not wanting to miss out on the gift of motherhood.

According to Blake, she never gave up hope of finding out what happened to his sister, Caroline. Now that Alyssa was experiencing pregnancy and would soon be a mother, she was beginning to have a deeper understanding of Mrs. O'Connor's courage and her own mother's pain.

She made a promise right then and there to do whatever had to be done in order to keep her daughter safe from whoever was coming for her. Even if that meant making herself uncomfortable being around Blake's family. He was right. There was security at the ranch. No matter how his family felt about her, they'd accept her and protect her.

It was just the way O'Connors were made.

Chapter Fifteen

Blake pulled into the parking lot of the doctor's office. His buddy, Aaron Smith, was off duty but he'd been ready to slap on his holster and escort Blake with no questions asked after a quick text. Aaron parked next to Blake. No doubt, Liz had filled in a few of their buddies. Or, heck, maybe they figured it out on their own. Word traveled fast in law enforcement circles. The best part was the brotherhood he felt, much like at home on the ranch. He would miss the friends he'd made at Houston PD once this was over and he returned to the ranch full-time.

Taking care of Alyssa and the baby was his top priority. Once those two were safe, he could resume searching for the truth about what happened to Caroline. Digging around in a thirty-year-old case meant following a lot of dead trails. He knew the odds of solving a cold case. Until his father's death, there'd been no leads. Now, it was clear that Finn O'Connor had been killed while taking up the investigation on his own. His health condition—a condition he'd been keeping secret—would have taken him at some point. But he still had time until he started investigating.

Blake exited the vehicle, scanning the small lot. The doctor's office was in a stand-alone building, which made it easier to monitor people coming and going. A couple walked out. The woman was less pregnant than Alyssa but it was clear she had a bump. She had on a smile while her partner had a worried look.

"Twins," she said to the man escorting her.

Blake could only imagine what that would be like. No wonder the man looked like someone had just robbed his piggy bank. Twins also meant twice the cost of everything. He strode over to the passenger door and opened it once he was certain the area was secure.

Having backup was a godsend.

Blake, acting nonchalant, took a glance around as he opened the door for her and stepped aside. He clicked the key fob, locking his Jeep.

There wasn't anything out of the ordinary going on in the parking lot. Blake held out his arm, thinking Alyssa had been to this place countless times without him, without support. They made their way inside. Glancing around the waiting room, it seemed more like a couple's retreat considering every female had a partner.

Now, he really felt bad. He reminded himself there wasn't much he could do about her taking these appointments alone when he had no idea that he was going to be a father in the first place. And yet, part of him couldn't help but think he'd done something wrong for her not to trust him.

Had he said something to lead her in the direction that he would be anything but thrilled to find out they were having a baby?

He walked beside her to the glass partition, noticing that all the chairs in the waiting room were pairs. Someone immediately opened the window and smiled.

"Can I help you?" the receptionist asked with a smile.

"Alyssa Hazel for Dr. Kero."

"What time is your appointment?" she asked. The usual receptionist must be out today and since this one didn't have a name tag, Alyssa assumed she was filling in or new.

"Eleven o'clock."

The receptionist glanced at the clock.

"I'm early."

"Okay. Can I see your ID and insurance card?" the front desk person asked.

"Um, normally that wouldn't be a problem, but I seem to have misplaced my purse," she said.

Blake smiled at the receptionist, turning on the O'Connor charm. "I called ahead and spoke to someone by the name of Lorraine."

"She's the office manager." The woman's cheeks flamed as she smiled back at Blake. "I'm new here."

"You see, I explained the situation to Lorraine,

and she said it wouldn't be a problem since the nurses already know who my wife is." He'd picked up on the fact that she wasn't still using her married name, but he went out on a limb.

"Okay. No problem then." She looked at Alyssa again. "What did you say your name was again?"

"Hazel," she supplied.

The worker pulled a chart out from a stack. "I have it right here. Take a seat and someone will be with you in a moment." She glanced at the file, and then called them back. "Is this still a cash account?"

Alyssa started to answer but Blake cut in. "I'm responsible for all the medical bills. I'm her husband." He had no idea why it felt important to say that, but it did.

A hint of confusion passed behind Alyssa's eyes even as a small smile upturned the corners of her lips.

"They'll settle up at the end of the visit." The receptionist smiled again.

Alyssa led them to a pair of chairs nestled in the corner of the room.

"You didn't have to do that," she said after taking a seat.

"Offer to pay the bill? Yes, I did."

"Well, no, I didn't mean that, but that too."

"Oh, the part about being your husband?" He wasn't ready to jump into the role again. Not after the hurt he'd experienced. But they needed to learn how to work together if they were going to co-parent.

"Yes." Her cheeks flamed and it made her even more beautiful.

"Yes, I did." He started to say it was about protecting her in case someone at the office had a connection to Christopher or Jordan, but he didn't want her to feel like she was alone in this. Up until now, she had been. Granted, it had been her choosing. But, was it? If she believed she was protecting him in some way, then she'd put herself in a hard position to do it. "I wanted to pay you back in some small way."

"Because?"

"You said before that you have a strong feeling you hid the pregnancy from me to protect me. The divorce was to protect me. And you've been doing all this alone. Something—" he motioned toward all the pairs of seats "—people normally do with a partner or spouse."

"The feeling is no doubt stronger than anything I've felt. I can promise you that. But what if I'm remembering this all wrong?" She motioned toward her head. "I lost three days of my life. I had no idea how long I was in the closet until someone told me. I don't remember how I got in there in the first place. Clearly, big chunks of my memory are gone."

He started his protest when a head poked from behind the door next to the window. Instead of saying what was on the tip of his tongue, he held off.

"Alyssa." The nurse had on scrubs.

Blake followed Alyssa, who followed the nurse into a hallway that was more like a maze with little rooms that made him feel like a mouse searching for cheese. They stopped off long enough for Alyssa to give a urine sample and then stand on a scale.

The nurse walked them into a room and told Alyssa to undress. She pointed to a paper gown that was folded and waiting on a bench. There was a privacy curtain that Alyssa ducked behind while Blake took a seat in one of the chairs against the same wall as the door.

The nurse busied herself on the laptop.

Alyssa pulled the curtain back after a few minutes. Seeing her look like a patient struck a chord with him. He also realized, ready or not, a baby was coming. He needed to pull up his bootstraps and be the partner she needed while they navigated the last part of the pregnancy and then the birth.

"In or out? It's your call," Alyssa said to Blake.

"YOU CAN STAY. If you don't think it would be too much," the nurse added. The table was positioned facing the opposite wall, so his chair was at her head and not the other way around. She figured it was strategic placement on her doctor's part.

He laughed. "Don't take this the wrong way, but I did grow up on a ranch. Birth is the most natural thing. So, no, nothing that happens in here could throw me for a loop."

"Okay. Because I've seen guys being wheeled out of here who apparently fainted when they saw what goes on," the nurse said.

"I'm good. Not even the sight of blood causes any distress. I'm pretty sure I've seen it all." He paused for a minute and then turned to Alyssa. "The thought of someone inflicting pain on you, on purpose or as part of an exam, doesn't do good things to my blood pressure. But—"

A knock at the door interrupted him.

"Come in," Alyssa said.

Dr. Kero stepped in, hands full with Alyssa's file. She looked to Alyssa, greeted her and then noticed Blake. She introduced herself and shook his hand after tucking the folder under her arm. After a quick hand wash later, she sat on her stool and then scooted it forward.

"Who have we brought with us today?" Dr. Kero asked with a smile.

"I'm her husband."

Was it wrong she liked hearing the sound of those words coming from Blake? Despite the need for them to work out how this was going to go once the baby arrived, she liked the fact her daughter was going to be surrounded by so much love. Being an O'Connor would give her a stable of uncles and aunts. A few cousins to grow up with. She wouldn't have any of those things on Alyssa's side of the family.

"So, I'm guessing this is the baby's father." Dr. Kero clasped her hands in her lap. She was good at giving her full attention to Alyssa during exams. The doctor had come highly recommended and it was easy to see why. Her bedside manner had a calming effect.

"That's right." Alyssa beamed. She couldn't help it.

Blake was incredibly hot. Top to bottom, the kind of good-looking that belonged on billboards. But it was his easy charm that disarmed people. It didn't hurt that the wattage in his smile was bright enough to light up the block. His smile was a show of perfectly straight, white teeth. And then there were his lips.

But she wasn't there to discuss Blake's good looks.

"I'm told you've been having cramps," the doctor continued without missing a beat.

"That's right."

"On a scale of one to ten, how would you describe them?"

"They've gone as high as an eight. No set pattern, though. We tried to time them. It didn't do any good."

"I like hearing that. It's a little early. We want to keep this angel in a few more weeks if possible." Dr. Kero's smile warmed her face—a face framed by shoulder-length dark hair and filled with big brown eyes. "Is Dad okay staying in the room while I perform an exam?"

"Yes." Alyssa hadn't thought much about going to these appointments alone, despite everything being set up for pairs. She never let the paired-up chairs in the lobby bother her. She'd never used the extra chair in the exam room for more than a place to stick her purse. And she'd never felt a bone-deep sadness about being here alone. So, the joy that filled her having Blake in the room caught her completely off guard. There was no question her feelings for him still ran deep. It was taking this appointment to tell her how much she'd missed him.

The doctor performed her exam.

At one point, Alyssa winced. Blake reached over and took her hand in his. He brought hers up to his lips and pressed a tender kiss there. The moment was so intimate she almost forgot about the pain of the exam.

"All done. You did great." The doctor wheeled her chair back, took off the gloves and deposited them in a metal receptacle.

"This time hurt more than the others. Is everything all right?"

The doctor nodded before listening to the baby's heartbeat. When she was done, she put her hand out and said, "You can sit up now."

Alyssa took her feet out of the stirrups and pushed up to sitting with some effort.

The doctor reclaimed her seat and positioned it in between Alyssa and Blake. "Here's the situation. You've dilated to two centimeters. I'm putting you on bed rest. I want you off your feet as much as possible and I want you to call me if you experience any cramping like you did yesterday."

Alyssa's mind reeled. There was still so much to do. She needed to go to her apartment. She needed to check her laptop. She was in the middle of an investigation. How on earth was she going to relax with everything going on?

"I—um—guess I wasn't expecting this," she stammered.

"It's a precaution. I don't want to take any chances with this little one. She's a little too eager to come out and I'd like to get a couple more weeks at the least of keeping her snug." The compassion on the doctor's face couldn't quell the panic squeezing Alyssa's chest.

"But all other signs are good?" Blake chimed in.

"So far, so good. We have a strong heartbeat and that's a good sign. Even if this little one comes early, girls' lungs typically develop faster than boys. Even so, we'd have NICU ready to go."

"Can I travel?" Alyssa asked.

"Are there any extenuating circumstances I need to know about?"

"Like?" Alyssa didn't want to tell her doctor scary men might be after her.

"Terminally ill relative would top my list. I might make an exception depending on the situation."

"No. Nothing like that."

"Then, I'd rather you be home. Comfortable. Feet up. And only move to go to the bathroom. Basically, you're a princess for the next couple of weeks." The doctor looked to Blake. "Think you can handle the assignment?"

"I got it." His jaw was set. His expression dead

serious. He had the kind of determination that said he'd move heaven and earth to take care of her.

And, granted, she could take care of herself just fine. She'd done so her entire life. But there was something incredible about someone else having her back again. She didn't realize how much she'd missed the connection they'd shared and the way each took care of the other.

It was obvious just how much her heart was going to break when she had to walk away from him a second time. Or, worse, have him in her life every day because of the baby but out of reach as a partner.

Chapter Sixteen

"Tell me what's on your mind." Blake could feel if not see the tension radiating from Alyssa after the exam. He navigated onto the road, figuring the ranch was out of the equation. They needed to decide where to go next but right now he figured she just needed him to drive.

With Aaron tailing them, he was reasonably certain he could keep them safe. Of course, he could drive her straight to the station. She'd be safe there. Unless someone was working from the inside. They needed to tell her mother they weren't coming to pick her up after all and that one of his brothers would. He needed to discuss this with Alyssa, but it wasn't safe for her mother to be with the two of them for the time being.

Alyssa issued a sharp sigh. He'd leaned her chair back as the doctor had instructed to make sure she didn't put too much pressure on her body while sitting upright. When the doctor said bed rest, she meant it in the strictest sense. She wanted Alyssa on her side as much as possible.

"I'm frustrated that I can't go to the ranch." It was hours away and she needed to be closer to her doctor just in case the baby decided to come early.

"Understandable."

"The security there would help me feel safer and I'm tired. I'm tired of not being able to remember much about the past eight months. I'm tired of not knowing who is after me and why. And I'm tired of not being able to walk across the street without worrying about someone named Bus Stop or the Judge erasing my life or threatening my child." She stopped herself like she needed a minute to gather her thoughts before continuing. She took in a few deep breaths. "And all this stress isn't good for the baby, but I'm struggling with calming down. There's no off button for the stress of basically running for your life while trying to relax for the benefit of your baby."

He didn't answer or try to offer solutions. She was finally talking to him and he figured she needed him to listen, to hear what she was saying rather than jump in and throw out a lot of words meant to fix things. She was intelligent and knew her own mind. In this moment, she needed to talk it through.

Blake navigated onto the highway, figuring being on a crowded road was safer than side streets. He could slide in and around traffic. Plus, there was no shortage of trucks, SUVs and Jeeps on a Houston highway, so it was easy to blend in.

"And I don't want to put you in more danger than I already have. I mean, those guys figured out where you live and came for me at a cop's house. What does that tell you about them? That takes a lot of stupidity."

"Or they didn't have a choice. They might have been up against a wall. Either they come for us or they end up dead."

"Well, they ended up dead anyway. So…"

"What happened to them wasn't your fault." She needed to know that. He didn't want her blaming herself for their actions.

"Why does it feel like everything is my fault then?"

"You care. Deeply. It's one of the reasons I fell in love with you. You're passionate and when you get something in your mind, you really go for it. You go all in." His words seemed to be soothing her. She'd loosened her grip on the seat belt strap. His chest filled with pride in the fact he could offer comfort. "You're also really hard on yourself. And you go all in on that too."

She leaned her head back and studied him.

"You noticed all that about me?"

"Yeah." He smiled. "Why wouldn't I?"

"I don't know. I guess I never really thought you were paying attention."

"I could have been better about telling you. What

you were talking about a minute ago. The part about holding your stress inside. I never wanted to bring mine home from the job. So, I didn't talk on rough days. It got easier and easier to keep quiet in general. And when you were dealing with your father's illness and then death, I let you go quiet too. It was a mistake on my part."

"There were two of us in that marriage. I only remember it being amazing."

"And it was for a couple of years. But then you needed me, and I didn't know what to do, so I lost you."

"That's not how I remember it happening."

"I'm not ready to let myself off the hook either. There were two of us in the marriage. It took both of us to make it work and that meant when I saw you struggling, I should have done more to help figure it out. That's all."

"We both share the blame?"

"That's how I see it."

She seemed to need to process the thought. She took her time, pinching the bridge of her nose like she was trying to stem a headache. He put on a classical music station. The soft music played in the background, low and soothing.

"That's nice." She reached over and touched his arm. "Thanks for everything you said."

"I meant every word."

"I know. That's what makes it special."

"You're welcome." He was true to his convictions.

He hadn't seen the situation as clearly before. He'd been too busy tending to his bruised ego after she'd walked out. But he should've seen the writing on the wall. Once they stopped communicating, it was only a matter of time before the rest would break down. She'd just seemed to be slipping into a deeper hole of sadness and he'd had no idea what to do.

They'd been driving for more than a half hour. He took the next exit and banged a U-turn at the first stop light. Instead of pulling back onto the highway, he pulled into the first gas station he could find and parked.

"Do you have a place to go in mind?" he asked. "I can request a safehouse but I can't make any guarantees of what that would look like."

"Good question. I doubt we can go back to your place. Not and expect to stay safe for long. My apartment will be watched as well. They have to know where I live."

"I didn't think about it before, but we can send Liz to your place to pick up your laptop. She can see if your handbag is there. Cell phone. All she would need is permission from your landlord."

"What about Aaron back there? Can he go instead?"

"You don't like Liz?"

"She's not my favorite person if I'm honest."

"I figured she irritated you. I didn't realize how strong your feelings were when it came to her."

"She knows a little too much about your every

move, Blake. Look, I'm not your wife anymore and it's clear she hates me for hurting you. I'm not even saying that I blame her. But I am saying that I don't want her in my home. Not if I have another choice."

"I'll have someone swing by in uniform. That way, your landlord will give access. Liz is already part of the investigation, but I'll keep her out as much as possible moving forward."

"It would be great if she didn't show up everywhere or look at me like she wants me dead."

"Liz looks at you like that?" He didn't doubt her, but he did want to make sure he heard her correctly.

"Afraid so."

"Then I'll find a way to do this without her."

"Where do we go from here?" Alyssa had been quietly coming at this new wrinkle in their plans—the doctor-ordered bed rest—from every angle for the past half hour before she and Blake finally spoke. She was practicing the deep breathing exercises her birthing teacher had taught her. Again, the woman deserved a hug, and a big one at that.

"We could always crash at a friend's place."

"And drag more innocent people into this mess? No way." She was already shaking her head the minute he suggested it.

"Fair enough."

She did realize he was talking about law enforcement officers who were used to putting their lives on the line. But that was their job. This was bringing their work home and possibly placing their families in danger.

"Is there a place where you think you'll be comfortable?" he asked. "A hotel? A furnished apartment? A vacation rental apartment?"

"I'd like to be as close to my doctor and the hospital as I can be in case we need to be there in a moment's notice. Something with a kitchen would be nice so we can cook."

He laughed.

"Oh, right. I'm not allowed to cook, am I?" Getting used to bed rest might be tricky.

"Not on my watch."

"Then we definitely need food readily available unless you've gone to cooking school in the past few months." She wanted to reel those last words in almost as soon as she spoke them, afraid she would hurt his feelings when she brought up anything about their recent history. He laughed and she sighed with relief. At least they were able to joke again and not feel like they had to constantly walk on eggshells. She'd take the progress.

Blake picked up his cell phone. He leaned over and asked, "Mind if I step out of the vehicle for a minute?"

"No." The question caught her off guard.

"I need to speak to my mother in private."

"Go right ahead." She tried to cover her surprise but figured she overcompensated with a goofy smile. She shouldn't let his request bother her. The man had a right to request to speak to his family without her right next to him. It still stung a little bit. Probably because she'd been part of that family in the past. They'd been nothing but good to her too and she realized how much she missed them. She'd forgotten or blocked out—she couldn't be certain which—just how much it hurt to be cut off from the family who'd so easily accepted her as one of their own.

He exited the Jeep and nodded toward Aaron, who was sitting in his vehicle with the engine idling nearby.

Alyssa leaned her head back again and focused on the deep breathing exercises she'd been taught. There was another trick. One that involved thinking the palms of her hands warm. She'd heard about it but never tried it. This seemed like as good a time as any to try something new. Decreasing her stress levels as much as possible was her second priority. Staying alive topped the list.

The door opened and Blake reclaimed his seat.

"How'd it go?" she asked.

"Good. We have a security team from home working on helping us out instead of the two of us trying to use this thing—" he held up his phone "—rather than a real computer."

"Some people claim a phone is all you need."

"You know me. I've never been a huge fan of staring at a screen all day. A computer comes in handy in police work and I have a laptop in my service vehicle."

"I can imagine there's a lot you can do with sharing information and such."

"It's staggering how dependent we are. But they're useful."

"How is your mother? I've been meaning to circle back to our conversation about your family."

"As good as can be expected." He lifted a shoulder casually but his tone was anything but relaxed.

"She and your dad were so close. They were literally everything I wanted to be in a marriage."

He cocked an eyebrow. "How so?"

"Your mother was always her own person. You know? She had her library. She did her own thing. She kept her independence, her sense of self despite having a large family. She and your dad always seemed like two perfect puzzle pieces fitting together. And, wow, could I use some parenting advice from her. All of her children are these truly amazing people." She stopped when she realized she was about to tell him what an incredible person he was, not wanting to gush. "Anyway, she always had this quiet strength that I admired."

He smiled.

"I've been thinking a lot about this little bean's name and I'd like it to represent something. I think her formal name could be Margaret, after her grandmother, but I'd like to call her Maggie. What do you think?"

"My mother would be honored." The look of admiration in his eyes reached deep inside her. It warmed her from the inside out that he appreciated the gesture.

"Does she know about the baby yet?"

He shook his head.

"Oh."

"I plan to tell her, of course. I just didn't want to do it over the phone in a situation like this. She'll be happy and want to celebrate."

"Will she?" She didn't mean to sound so surprised. It was just that she figured there wasn't an O'Connor who would actually welcome anything that had to do with her.

"You bet she will. You should see her face when she's around Cash's little girl. And, besides, everyone at the ranch could use good news for a change. We need something to celebrate."

That, she understood.

"And, speaking of the ranch, you should know that I plan to tender my resignation at work once we get you out of trouble." Hearing those words truly shocked her.

"I thought you loved your work." She was pretty certain her mouth was agape.

"It's the right time." Blake's cell buzzed. He glanced at the screen and an address popped up in his text messages.

"We have a house by the hospital," he said. "And don't worry, it'll meet all your criteria."

"Okay, but we're talking about your career plans once we get there." She didn't want to drop the subject and she didn't want to be the one responsible for him leaving a career he loved. He would resent her for the rest of his life if he gave up something he was so passionate about. And after everything that had happened between them, she definitely didn't want that to be the case.

Chapter Seventeen

The house should be classified as a mansion. The streets of the gated community were flanked by rows of perfectly manicured palm trees, tall and majestic. Houston had always had a tropical vibe with its palm trees, but the driveway to the house seemed more like a botanical garden.

"Are you kidding me right now?"

"I wouldn't kid you," he said with a laugh.

A quick glance at Alyssa and all he could see were those big gorgeous eyes of hers—wide open and trying to take in the magnificence.

"Who lives here?" she asked.

"A prominent Houston quarterback," he said.

Aaron followed closely behind, and he seemed just as shocked.

What could Blake say? His family was the O'Connors of Texas. They were as down-to-earth as they could be, so it was easy to forget his parents had friends in very high places and connections around the entire state, not to mention a private security team. Hell, he came from high places even though he'd never felt rich one day in his life. Money was a means to an end for ranchers, and not the central focus of their lives. They were practical people who valued hard work and honesty over zeroes in a bank account.

So, it was easy to forget about the one's in Blake's. And when he really thought about it, which he didn't normally, there were quite a few.

Another longer text came through as he parked in the circular drive in front of an all-brick two-story that put his own parents' house to shame. This place had two distinct wings and had to be more than twenty-thousand square feet.

"Holy cow," Alyssa said.

There was no visible security and at a place like this there had to be a sophisticated system with someone watching over the place.

He glanced at his phone after parking. He scanned the text. Alarm code? Check. And, yes, there was on-site security. The owners, a prominent Houston quarterback and his new wife, were on the road and wouldn't be home for weeks.

"There are sensors everywhere outside and more security than Fort Knox. No one's getting in here undetected," he explained.

Aaron parked and then came to the driver's side, arms out wide and a look of disbelief planted on his face.

Blake rolled down the window and held up his left wrist. "You never saw my Rolex before, man?"

Aaron gave a smile and a wave to Alyssa that warmed Blake's heart, especially after he learned how Liz had been making Alyssa feel.

Yes, his former partner had had a ringside seat to his pain. He even understood a little bit of protectiveness on Liz's part. There was no reason to go overboard. Blake made his own decisions and his friends respected it. Hell, it was the same going the other way. If one of his buddies got back together with an ex, Blake might warn him or her, but he would never make the ex feel uncomfortable around him. That would be uncool. Behind closed doors, he might make his concern known.

"I know you don't live in this house because I've seen it featured on one of those shows that bring you into athletes and celebrity homes. A certain famous quarterback lives here. It looks even bigger in person than it did on the TV." Aaron was obviously impressed. Blake needed to tell Alyssa to remind him not to invite any of his buddies to the ranch. Granted, the house wasn't this impressive, but it was grand. Only once or twice did his last name come up and a joke about him being one of the richest men in Texas. The conversation always ended with someone shaking their head and saying a rich boy would never put his life on the line every day for strangers.

"Lucky for you that you volunteered to help me out then. Because this is where we're staying for the next couple of days until we figure out who Bus Stop and the Judge are." His cell buzzed. He checked the screen. Liz. He'd call her back in a few minutes.

"Darn straight I'm lucky. Doing a favor has never paid off like this." Aaron's eyes would never be wide enough to fully take in this scene. His reaction might be funny, but the threat against Alyssa was no laughing matter.

"Shall we?" He motioned toward the massive double doors.

"Hell, yeah. I can't wait to see what's inside."

Blake hopped out of the driver's seat and was around to the passenger side a second too late. Aaron already had the door open and was helping Alyssa out. This visual shouldn't disturb Blake as much as it did. He wanted to be the one she leaned on.

Shaking off the thought, he moved to the keypad next to the door and punched in the first code of the smart house. A click sounded to his right. Ta-da. The front door was unlocked. He glanced up at the security camera above the door as it moved to snap a picture of the visitors. He had thirty seconds to get inside and to the keypad behind the door.

The next code did its trick. The system was disarmed in seconds. The others had already come inside the entryway.

"I just remembered something. My whole apartment could fit in here," Alyssa said, waving her arms around in the space ten steps inside the front door.

"Same," Aaron said walking over toward a table that had several footballs locked inside a lighted case.

"Don't touch anything," Blake warned.

"I'm not doing anything." Aaron's hands went up, palms out, in the surrender position.

"I know a guy who works security." Blake figured it was a white lie. He did know one of the men who worked here. He just wasn't the reason they were invited. "I don't want him to get into trouble for helping us out. That's all."

"Oh, man. This place is huge." Aaron shouted, "Hello," and there was literally an echo.

Blake preferred a cozy place, nothing more than a great room, decent kitchen, and two or three bedrooms. This was over-the-top on every level. He didn't want to need an intercom to speak with his wife from across the house.

The home looked worthy of an old *MTV Cribs* episode. The best way to describe the decorating style was white and minimalist. The floors were white marble. The walls were painted some type of white. Probably something like eggshell if he had to guess. The furniture in the adjacent living room was white. As he walked the long entryway, he saw that the furniture in the dining room was also white. There were a few colorful pieces here and there. Mostly art. Like in the dining room, there was a huge red dot on a framed canvas. He wasn't a fancy-enough eater to sit on an all-white chair. His two main meals of tacos and barbecue wouldn't cut it on those seats.

"I'd say make yourselves comfortable but I'm afraid to sit down anywhere in here," he said. He checked his phone for the location of a master remote. Apparently, there were two and they ran the entire house, security and all.

"I don't have anything better to do but my question is this. Do you still need me with all this extra security?" Aaron asked.

"Not really. We'll be here overnight at the least. I think we're safe here."

"Can I take a look around before I head out?"

"Let's grab a tour."

If ALYSSA LIVED to be a hundred, she would probably never see anything as grand as this home ever again. The movie room was literally a replica of a small theatre. There was a game room that had four pinball machines, which was her favorite game. And a bowling alley.

The room was a sports fan's dream. A wall of flat screens on the back wall. A fully stocked bar to the left, complete with leather stools. The kind of sectional sofa that she could literally sink into and maybe never get out of anchored the room. And there were throw blankets everywhere she looked.

She imagined being curled up on the sofa, watching a movie with Blake. Forget the movie theatre in the opposite wing with its popcorn and candy bar along with lounge chairs. She would never leave this room if she lived here.

Once the tour ended, Aaron said his goodbyes before taking off. Blake had located one of the remote controls that apparently ran everything. It was the size of a laptop. He armed the alarms, a stark reminder they weren't here for the toys.

"Do you want to lie down in the guest room?" There was more than one, but she knew he was talking about the closest one off the kitchen. It was most likely a mother-in-law suite complete with a walk-in closet larger than Alyssa's bedroom at home.

"Can I stay in there?" She motioned toward the TV room.

"You can go anywhere you think you'll be more comfortable as long as you agree to lie down." His smile shouldn't cause a dozen butterflies to take flight in her stomach, but it did.

"Scouts honor." She walked into the room and just as she'd expected, sank into the sectional. There were dozens of pillows, so she placed a few around herself and got comfortable. Other than showering and going to the bathroom, she would be on her side or her back for the foreseeable future.

Blake sat down next to her.

"One of the guys picked up a few of your personal things from the house and Liz intercepted him. She wants to bring them herself."

"Oh."

"I can have someone else bring them over." His concern touched her deeply. The way he'd snapped into protective mode had her heart wishing things had turned out differently between them. As it was, they needed to learn to co-parent, not be a couple. Besides, would he ever fully trust her again after what happened?

"No. It's okay." It wasn't, and Alyssa still wasn't thrilled about Liz, but the woman seemed like she was trying to help.

"Are you sure?" His face twisted.

"Yes. I still don't like her personally. But she's trying to be helpful."

"She's on her way." He needed to let security know Liz was coming. "In the meantime, you must be hungry. What sounds good?"

"I'd pretty much take anything at this point," she admitted. "Food does sound really good."

"The fridge is supposed to be stocked. Let's see what we can work with."

She reached out and touched his hand. The electricity nearly caused her to pull hers back.

"Thank you, Blake."

His fact twisted up again.

"For what?"

"Taking care of us. You don't have to do this."

"That's where you're wrong, Alyssa. It's my responsibility as much as yours." It made sense that he was going out of his way for the safety and well-being of his child. And yet, hearing it put that way stung just a little bit. Good to know where she stood, though.

"While you deal with Liz and find food, I'd like

to take a nap." Alyssa hugged a pillow to her chest and tucked her feet behind her. She'd already kicked off her shoes when she first sat down on the sofa.

"Okay." It felt like a wall had just come up between them and a lot like she'd stepped on a landmine. He pushed to standing and started walking away.

In the past, she would have sucked it up and let it be. Maybe it was the fact that dangerous men were chasing her, but she didn't want to stuff her feelings down deep this time. "Hey, Blake."

"Yes." He turned around.

"I don't know what just happened here but don't freeze me out. Okay?"

"Is that what you think I'm doing?"

"Seems so."

"In case you haven't noticed, I still care about you a helluva lot," he started.

"And you have every right to protect this baby."

"Things between us are more complicated than that."

"Which is why I don't want to sweep this under the rug. I appreciate the fact you asked me about Liz. But I'm not sure what happened after that conversation was over," she admitted.

"I'm trying to figure out the boundaries here, Alyssa. I realize that I've only recently found out about the baby. I'm sure once I see her, I'll be head over heels. But right now, all I have to go on is how I felt about you and it's throwing me for a loop."

"I agree that we need to find common ground."

"And I do realize the kisses have to stop. They aren't helping me with perspective." Now, he just looked torn. He stabbed his fingers in his hair. "It's just not easy to go from loving you with all my heart, to coming to terms with our divorce, to finding out we're about to have a child together."

"Agreed on the kisses no matter how much I enjoyed every one of them." She jutted her chin out, determined to let him know he wasn't the only one battling going for what she wanted versus thinking about what might make them better co-parents to their child. "And I never expected for this pregnancy to happen. It caught me off guard and it's taken me a while to connect with this little bean. But it helps that she's growing inside me and I can feel her move." The little one picked that moment to kick.

"She did it just now, didn't she?" His gaze went to her belly because the baby kicked so hard her shirt moved.

"Yes. And it was a doozy." Alyssa thought he was doing pretty well all things considered. "Hey, for what's it's worth, you're doing great with all this. You've had hours to figure this out on no notice with someone I'm pretty much guessing you never thought you'd see again. Does that about sum up the situation?"

"I have to admit. You did a pretty good job right there."

His cell buzzed in his hand. No doubt, it was Liz. He checked the screen. "I should answer this text."

"Okay."

He started to walk into the next room but stopped halfway there.

"It's good that we're talking through this, Alyssa. It's progress." At this point, that was all she could ask for.

Chapter Eighteen

I'm out front.

The text from Liz came quicker than Blake expected. He chalked it up to being distracted as he stood in front of the double fridge doors trying to figure out what to fix for dinner. Thankfully, there were a few frozen pizzas. No salad or fruit since the homeowners were traveling. It wouldn't make sense to have those. There was plenty of everything else if Alyssa didn't mind frozen meals for a few days. He could always run out for fresh food to make it a little healthier.

He disarmed the alarm using the remote. It was the biggest remote he'd ever seen. There was a feature that unlocked the front door as well. First, he checked the camera to make sure Liz hadn't brought anyone with her.

He'd told her to wait in the vehicle, but she was at the front door holding the items she'd promised. He stopped long enough to take in her body language.

She was looking up at the camera, tapping her foot impatiently.

Was she in a big hurry?

Blake strode over to the door and then opened it.

"Hey." The look in her eyes was patient and something else. Something he was having trouble pinpointing. Nervous? Nah. Couldn't be that.

"Thanks for bringing these by." He took the items as Liz glanced around him. Was she looking for Alyssa? His first thought was that Liz might have something to say that she didn't want Alyssa to hear.

"You're welcome."

"Anything else?" he asked.

"No. Same. Great place here. This belong to a friend of yours?" Again, she glanced up at the camera.

"I know the security guard." He shook his head. "Family is out of town for a few days."

"This place belongs to that famous football player, doesn't it?"

He shrugged, figuring he didn't need to hear any teasing about it later. Of course, he'd already made up his mind to leave the force. He had vacation days saved, so he could call in once this was settled. His time on the streets was over. He and Liz had been close at one time. Like brother and sister. So, why didn't he suddenly want to reveal his plans?

"Thanks for stopping by and bringing these. I owe you a few for all this," he said to her.

"Yeah. No problem. I know you'd do the same for

me if I needed it." She looked at him strangely. Like she expected him to ask her to come inside.

"I need to get back to it." He brought the door close to his body, essentially blocking her view of the inside of the house. "Thanks again."

"Right." She took a step back and then glanced at the camera again. "I'll let you know if anything comes up on the murders."

"All right then. Drive safe." It was an odd thing to say and yet he'd run out of *thank-yous*. He closed the door and then grabbed the remote off the table where he'd set it before opening the door. He watched the camera and got one of those weird feelings as Liz walked to her car. After locking the door and making sure the area was secure, he fished his cell phone out of his pocket and called Aaron.

"What's up?" Aaron was all business. He was also a mutual friend of Blake's and Liz's.

"Everything's good. I just have a question and it may come off as out of the blue." He couldn't help but feel like he was missing something with Liz.

"Shoot."

"You've been around Liz."

"Yeah, we've been friends for a long time. Why?"

"Ever notice anything different when she was around me than with other officers?" He was tap dancing around the subject.

"Like, what? The fact that she took a shine to you?"

"When you say shine, do you mean—"

"She had it for you bad. It was plain as the nose on my face. Why? Did she finally make a move? Because her timing couldn't be worse if you ask me." The way he spoke about the crush she had like he was reading last year's news made Blake realize how obvious it must have been to everyone but him.

"No. No move. Nothing like that. Alyssa mentioned Liz has given her the cold shoulder and I couldn't figure out why."

"Now you know. Liz pined over you after..." His voice trailed off and Blake knew exactly what he was referring to. The divorce. "But it's all good. She hasn't said anything in a long time. Not that she ever confided in me about her love life. I could just tell by the way she talked about you and especially Alyssa. So, I'm not surprised Liz hasn't exactly been easy on her."

"I didn't just miss the boat on that one, I didn't even see the ship in the harbor."

Aaron laughed. "It's all water under the bridge now, right? I mean, you and Alyssa are getting back together and starting a family."

"The only thing we're planning right now is figuring out how to be parents together. That's enough for the time being." He didn't feel a lot of conviction in those words. There was a whole lot going on in the back of his mind when it came to his relationship with Alyssa. Part of him was waiting for the truth to come out. If she'd left him to protect him like she mentioned, like she'd convinced herself, could he give their relationship a second chance?

Not without change. Not without knowing she would come to him to talk about a problem rather than try to solve it herself, leaving him in the dark. Relationships didn't work that way. Clearly.

"Whatever you want. You know I'm here for you."

"Thanks. Same if you ever need a favor." Blake would miss Aaron.

They exchanged goodbyes and ended the call.

How had Blake missed something right under his nose? If Aaron had picked up on it, others had to have too. Was that also the reason she was going above and beyond on the investigation? Was she hoping to win him over?

The last thing he wanted to do was give her false hope because he would only ever see her as a buddy, as a sister figure. There could never be more between them and it had nothing to do with Alyssa, who was more his type. He was attracted to intelligence. It was the first thing he noticed about someone once he got past the external. Then it was sense of humor. Strength and vulnerability. Too many people confused being strong with never showing their flaws. On the contrary, it was flaws that made a person unique. Perfectly imperfect. Easy to see and yet hard to pinpoint. Alyssa had the kind of strength that allowed her to be vulnerable to someone, to Blake.

He could never see himself with someone who didn't value family. His was at the center of his world despite the fact he hadn't been showing it in recent years. He'd become obsessed with finding out what happened to his sister. Then the job had taken on a life of its own, keeping him busy and tired. The search got harder and he went home less often. His biggest regret would be not spending more time with his father in his last years.

Blake had no plans to repeat the same mistake when it came to his mother. He needed to have a conversation with Alyssa about where their child would be brought up and how. His head started spinning with questions that would need answers. Since easy answers wouldn't come, he needed to regroup. They had a little time before the baby came to get on the same page, but the amount of decisions that needed to be made were already mind-numbing.

Picking up the remote and Alyssa's belongings, he hoped she'd find some answers on her laptop. Or at least a better direction. They had plenty of resources on this case and didn't seem to be making any progress. So far, they'd been one step behind. And for the first time in Blake's professional career, he didn't know how to turn it around.

ALYSSA MUST'VE NODDED off again. She woke to the smell of pizza. Pepperoni. Pushing up, she saw movement out of the corner of her eye.

"Hey." Alyssa's voice had the rough, sleepy quality.

"Did I wake you?" he asked.

"Nah." She sat up.

"Are you hungry?" He was by her side in two steps, offering an arm for her to leverage and pull herself up.

"Starving. If the pizza tastes half as good as it smells, I'll be in heaven."

"It's ready and waiting."

She pulled herself up to standing, and then took off down the hallway where she remembered seeing a bathroom. A person could easily get lost in a house this large, so she figured she would stick to the couple of rooms she knew.

After using the facilities and washing up, she joined Blake in the kitchen.

He shook his head the minute she entered the room.

"Right. Bed rest." She rubbed her belly. Slowing down wasn't going to come naturally to her by any means. She'd always been on the go.

This was important and nothing mattered more than her baby's health, so off to the TV room she went.

Blake joined her with two plates. He handed one over and produced a bottle of water that had been tucked underneath his arm.

"You didn't eat yet?"

"I waited."

"You must be starving."

He smiled. "I could eat."

The next few minutes were spent in silence, another sign of just how hungry they both were. Once he set his empty plate on the coffee table, he retrieved a drink for himself from a mini fridge in the corner of the room.

"I owe you an apology," he said.

"For what?"

"Liz," he started. "I don't know if I've misled her in some way, but I definitely didn't get the memo about her wanting more than a friendship until it was pointed out to me. I never would have brought her around you if I'd known that was the case."

"You finally picked up on that, huh?" It had been painfully obvious to Alyssa and she'd gotten jealous despite not having any right to.

"We just didn't see our friendship in the same light." He motioned toward a couple of objects on the massive coffee table. "She dropped those off earlier."

"My purse. And my laptop." Those would come in handy. She had a quick thought about seeing if her passport was in her wallet. Maybe a trip out of the country was in order. Then, she glanced down at her belly and remembered that she couldn't even go more than a handful of miles away from the hospital.

At least she could log into her work files and dig around. Something told her to log in using her father's credentials. He'd given them to her in case she got locked out trying to use her own. After finishing up the last of the water bottle, she grabbed her laptop and booted up the system.

Without knowing what she was looking for, this felt a lot like digging around for a needle in a haystack. Thinking of her dad reminded her of her mother.

"I should probably use your phone and check in on my mother," she said. Not having her cell made her anxious.

"She's on her way to the ranch. I texted Colton earlier and he arranged to have her picked up," Blake said. He checked his watch, which was not, by the way, a Rolex. "In fact, she might already be there by now. I'm guessing there haven't been any hiccups or I would have heard from one of my brothers by now."

"Thank you for taking care of her."

"Last I checked, you're still family." He seemed to regret those words as soon as they came out of his mouth. "I didn't mean what I said earlier about me only helping because of the baby. Once family, always family in my book. I'm always available to help if you need me. I didn't make that clear before."

"It's fine. Our situation is…complicated."

"You could say that all right." His laugh was a low rumble. It was sexy and reminded her how long it had been since she'd been intimate with anyone.

That ship had sailed as far as she was concerned. Trying to date with a newborn in tow meant she was pretty much saying goodbye to any semblance of a love life for the foreseeable future. She would miss sex. She already did.

What was that saying? Can't throw out the baby with the bath water.

Why was anyone trying to throw out the baby in the first place? She laughed at her own internal joke.

Okay, she was getting campy. So, bed rest was going to be awesome. If by awesome she meant a nightmare.

"What am I looking for?" She refocused on the laptop.

"Finances are always a good bet. Shipping or logistics records is next."

"Dad was constantly in and out of Mexico for business." As a supplier to a popular chain of World Market–type fare, he was in and out of the country. He worked with a couple of suppliers near the border.

"What about known associates?"

"He took me to meet a couple of his contacts last year. He was pushing me to take over because he was thinking about retiring." Her parents needed an income to survive, so her father was grooming her to step into his shoes. He'd stay on part-time, but she would meet with the customers stateside. He joked she was young and pretty—the combination would get more orders than if they dealt with a decrepit old man.

"What did you think about the people you met?"

She shrugged. "They seemed nice. Nothing sticks out as out of the ordinary."

This was frustrating. The memories were right there, just out of reach. Did she have the answers to their questions locked inside her brain? Was the trauma the only reason she couldn't access the vault?

They were *her* thoughts for crying out loud. Who couldn't remember their own thoughts?

"Don't try to force it. You're not the only way to get to the information." He refrained from saying who was.

"Liz?"

"It's a little late to remove her from the case now."

"I wouldn't want to. I need all the help I can get. And, believe me, I realize she is only doing this to help you. But it's going to help me, so I won't complain. I'd prefer not to have to see her, but that's a whole different story."

At least he laughed this time. The two of them were on better footing. At the end of the day, that was all that mattered to her. It didn't hurt that he'd finally figured Liz out.

Liz?

Why did Alyssa have a bad feeling about the woman? This ran deeper than the situation with Blake.

She logged on to her father's email, skimming the names and subject lines. She ran a search for Mexico and found a vacation he'd been planning. Apparently, he was putting together a surprise trip for his anniversary. He'd had no idea how sick he would become or that pneumonia would leave his life feeling unfinished. He should have taken better care of himself. She'd gotten on him countless times for eating junk on the road when he drove back and forth across the border. And smoking.

"He'd been spending more time on the road before he got sick. I remember that now," she said. Bits and pieces were coming back to her.

"Could he have been having trouble with a supplier?"

She ran a search for the names of the business contacts she'd met. Jose Ramirez. Raul Espinosa. Alex Rodriguez. She skimmed their email exchanges. All the messages were polite. No sign of trouble in paradise.

Email was netting a big zero. Of course, if her father was involved in something illegal… Hold on. Her father had told her something. Had her sign something. What?

Trying to remember made her brain cramp.

She blew out a frustrated breath. "It's right there in my mind. Why can't I access it?"

"It'll come. I know this is easier said than done but if you try not to focus on it, the answer might come to you."

"I've given that same advice dozens of times. Being on the other end of it doesn't feel so great." In fact, she decided right then and there never to utter those words again. She wasn't mad at Blake. He was trying to help. He was also right even though it didn't help with her frustration. And it wasn't like she could take a walk or exercise to work off some of the tension she felt. Bed rest.

She pecked away at the keyboard of her laptop, pulling up the most recent balance sheet. *Hmm.*

There was nothing out of the ordinary there. What about the bank account? Blake made a good point when he mentioned money. If something illegal was going on, money was a good place to start looking for a trail.

She logged on to the corporate bank account and searched for any sizeable withdrawals. Theirs was a small office, consisting of an administrative assistant, who was basically a jack-of-all-trades, and a customer service representative who was more problem solver than anything else. Trish Callum had been her father's right hand and he'd hired her niece for the customer service job two years ago. Delaney Rhinehart was a single mother to a four-year-old boy.

Being a small family office, everyone got along, which didn't necessarily mean there weren't secrets. Still, wouldn't Alyssa know if either were involved in illegal activity? And even if they were, why come after Alyssa? Why not go after one of them?

She decided neither one was involved or knew anything about her father's activities despite Trish having worked for her father for almost ten years. She stayed in her lane, helping set up computer files and making sure documents made it into the appropriate folder. She helped keep the office running smoothly. Besides, no alarms sounded when Alyssa thought of either of those two. Her father, however, was another story.

When she thought of him, a warning flared deep in her chest.

"I'm not seeing anything strange going on with money." Her eyes stopped on a withdrawal the minute she said that. "Hold on."

Blake moved beside her, causing her heart to hammer a little faster against her rib cage. Heat climbed up her neck, spreading to her cheeks. She could feel the flush as it crawled over her. So much for not giving away her body's reaction to him.

"See this." She pointed to the screen.

"That's a sizeable cash withdrawal."

"I didn't see anything like this on the balance sheet." She pulled it up again for reference. She'd learned not to take her memory for granted here in the third trimester when she could literally walk into a room and forget why. Granted, those incidents happened to everyone at times. For her, it was happening regularly.

A cramp stopped her cold. She did the breathing technique she'd been taught and was able to manage the pain.

"This little munchkin seems determined to show up early," Blake said. The term was endearing. "Asking if you're okay seems like it qualifies as a stupid question."

"It was a little rough but seems to be calming down now." For the second time in the last five minutes, she needed to eat her words.

Alyssa gasped and grabbed Blake's hand, wishing he could stop the pain threatening to consume her. Was this baby about to force her way into the world?

Chapter Nineteen

Blake couldn't remember the last time he'd felt helpless and useless at the same time. Watching Alyssa suffer through another cramp brought on both full tilt. She breathed her way through the pain, and he figured she was the bravest person in the room.

"What can I do?" he asked, impressed by her calm demeanor considering she was in an enormous amount of pain, and how willing she seemed to do whatever it took to keep the baby safe.

"For a second there, I thought we might be making a trip to the hospital." She let go of his hand and rubbed her belly. "I'm not ready to make the call just yet."

"You're going to be an amazing mother." He couldn't keep the awe out of his voice.

"How do you know?"

"It's obvious to me how much you love her already. You're warm and compassionate. You're devoted to her. She's going to be one lucky kid."

The flush to her cheeks made her even more beautiful but he wasn't trying to embarrass her.

"Thank you, Blake. It means a lot to hear you say that. Especially after…" Her voice trailed off and was filled with so much regret at those last words.

"Water under the bridge," he quickly countered.

"Really?"

"As far as I'm concerned."

"Even though—"

"I have no interest in looking back or measuring mistakes. I especially don't care to point fingers or assign blame. What's in the past is in the past. I don't know about you but I'm ready to move forward." He wasn't asking her to forget the past and neither would he. He was far more interested in learning from it, and then moving on. "We have a child to get ready for. You were right about our situation being complicated before. There's no denying it with our history."

Her lips compressed like she was stopping herself from saying something.

"That same history allows us to know each other. I realize it's not the same. Before, it was like we could read each other's thoughts. That's asking too much now. Because of our past, I know you like long drives on the property. Your favorite color is green, the exact color of grass. You love peperoni pizza and would trade your family business for a good fish taco."

At least that comment brought out a smile.

"I know how hard you work and that you're going

to need support to bring up this child. You're responsible for your mother and your family business employs family who depend on their paychecks and enjoy working together."

She nodded and he could almost see the wheels turning in her mind.

"You like to sleep late," he pointed out. "But only on Sundays. And you like to stay in bed as long as possible. I caught you pretending to be asleep so you wouldn't have to get up before you were ready."

"How did you know?"

"Your breathing. There's a certain sound you make when you're sleeping."

"Snoring?" Her cheeks flushed again.

"No. More like a steady, even rhythm. Like a really good George Strait song."

Now, she smiled, and it chipped away at his resolve.

"And you know me too."

"That's right." Her eyes sparkled. "I sure do. I know how much you like crispy beef tacos and that you love family above all else. Your favorite color is blue like the night sky. And that's your favorite thing to look at despite the fact you start yawning after eight o'clock on your nights off. You say you don't care for children, but I've seen a little spark in your eye when you pass by a curly-haired angel."

"No one said I didn't care for children. I said I didn't much like 'other' people's children," he defended, quirking a smile.

She laughed.

"You wake up so early on your days off it's crazy. And you like to jump right out of bed and get in a workout."

"That's the hazard that comes with growing up on a ranch."

"You're all tough on the outside but you care deeply. About everyone who gets close to you. So much so, that you sometimes have blinders on when you're around them."

She had him there. Case in point, Liz.

"And I know you're thinking Liz right now but I'm also talking about me. You think I'm a better person than I am because I have a bad feeling that I did something wrong and I can't pinpoint why."

"Something you needed to protect me from?" he asked.

"There's where I draw a frustrating blank." She locked gazes with him. "Whatever it was, I have a feeling I was covering for myself. What if I know Bus Stop or the Judge personally? Maybe I should just make myself visible. They wanted information from me. Or wanted me to talk. I'm not sure why but I get the feeling I was doing something wrong."

"With your father?"

"No idea if Dad was involved. Something tells me the answer is yes."

"That puts us right back at the beginning." He still didn't believe she would knowingly and willingly do anything illegal. He'd heard about businesses having trouble getting products in and out of Mexico over the past few years. Corruption was rampant with government officials there. "I just had an idea. Do you think it's possible the cash withdrawal was for a bribe to get goods out of the country and into the US?"

"Warning bells are sounding in my head when you talk about it."

"I have another thought if you want to hear it."

"Yes. I do." She quirked a brow.

"Extortion. Your father might have been paying someone off to move product out of Mexico."

"Would it be illegal for him to pay a person in another country if his supply chain broke down? Grease the wheels so to speak or pay for protection?"

"Not technically. Unless the men were extorting money from your father. That's another ballgame." The thought also occurred to him that she was trying to protect him. Would having her name dragged through the mud put Blake's job at risk? Dealing in the gray area as a business could lead to bad publicity. Doing something illegal could cost him his badge.

A picture was emerging that concerned him.

"What if the payments stopped?" he asked. "What if that's the reason they're after you."

"One of the guys mentioned something about getting me to talk. He was disturbed they were going to have to break or cut off my finger." She skimmed the bank account and he noticed similar transactions, all cash and none in the exact same amount. "These withdrawals happen every month, like clockwork. Different day and amount, but in the same range."

"If they were on the same day or the exact same amount, it would raise a red flag," he pointed out. "Varying the day and amounts makes it easier to slip under the radar. They're all less than ten thousand dollars too. So, no red flags to the feds. Can you click on one of them and verify it's your father?"

Just in case one his employees was taking the money.

She clicked on a transaction from last year and her father's signature was on the withdrawal slip.

"How about this one?" There shouldn't be any withdrawals after her father passed away.

Alyssa's face went bleached-sheet white. "How can that be?"

The name on the slip was Alyssa Hazel.

"It's me."

There was a long silence that followed Alyssa's words. Shock robbed her voice and her mind swirled. How could *she* be the one to pick up where her dad left off? And yet, now that she'd had a few minutes to let this news digest, she couldn't deny how familiar it felt. She glanced at the date shortly after her father's illness put him in the hospital.

Her signature.

She moved to the month before.

Her father's signature.

The month before that yielded the same result, her father. Her fingers guided the arrow to each date after her father's hospitalization. Her signature.

"You walked out shortly after your father's hospitalization. About the time you took over." Blake's voice was so low she almost couldn't hear him. "You said you were protecting me."

More of those puzzle pieces clicked together as he spoke. She expected him to look at her with disdain and found compassion instead.

"I don't know why I agreed to take over for him. It's obvious that's what I did, though."

"Save the family business. Take care of your mother. Keep an income coming in. Those are just the reasons off the top of my head," he said.

"Clearly, I was doing something illegal with the money. If anyone found out, I'd be easily connected to you as your wife. With your job in law enforcement, that would be the end of your career."

He nodded. "You could have been trying to save my life as well."

"It wouldn't surprise me."

"We don't know the reason for the payments. Could be to move legal products over the border," he said.

"But then what information could they possibly want from me?"

"That's the next step. Finding the answer."

A cramp nearly doubled her over. She breathed through it.

"What do you say to closing the laptop for the rest of the night? We're here. We're safe. We don't have to figure everything out all at once."

She managed to nod as a second cramp nearly knocked the wind out of her. She forced herself to focus on the breathing exercises as she felt Blake's hand on her back. The physical connection to him had a calming effect on her.

"Sounds like a good idea." Worst case scenario, the cramps continued, and they had to call her doctor or head over to the hospital. They were close to both.

"Does it help if I massage here?" He ran his hand along her lower back with the perfect amount of pressure.

"That feels amazing." It also gave her something to focus on besides the cramps. She felt a tightening in her stomach as well. Braxton Hicks contractions?

The thought of having contractions, false or otherwise, caused her to panic. Going through all this for the first time wasn't for the faint of heart. She also recognized the amount of stress she'd been under recently was most likely affecting her. Basically, she needed to find a way to chill out.

A movie? The big screen was tempting, and she couldn't remember the last time she'd curled up on the couch to watch TV. Figuring out how to turn it on and find a channel would be the tricky part. She motioned toward the flat-screen. "Maybe we could watch something to take our minds off everything going on?"

"I'll grab the remote." He didn't miss a beat getting up and locating it on the coffee table. It was another smart device. She figured this house was probably wired with more intelligence than she was.

After a few minutes, a full menu of movie options covered the screen.

"Something light or funny would be nice," she said.

He found several options. Apparently, there were entire channels for this sort of thing. She'd missed out on the binge-watch culture, preferring to read or work a good crossword puzzle. She listened to music for background noise. But, mostly, she worked. Taking over the family business from her father under extreme circumstances had been like drinking from a fire hose. She'd known a lot of the basics of running the day-to-day operations. But it was her father who handled all the financials. He was the one who made the visits, which she now realized was so he could hand off a bribe.

The movie they'd settled on wasn't fifteen minutes in when the next cramp hit. This was by far the worst one she'd experienced. The baby kicked and a sudden urge to use the restroom said the little angel had kicked Alyssa's bladder. Breathing through the pain barely made a dent.

"We should call the doctor," she finally conceded, grateful to have Blake with her.

He reached for the cell and she couldn't help but think how relieved he'd looked when they figured out what was going on with her family business. Did he also realize she'd never stopped loving him?

The next cramp told her something was definitely wrong.

Chapter Twenty

Go to the hospital.

Blake noted the doctor hadn't messed around on the call. It took her all of about half a second to make her declaration. Within two minutes, they were on the way to the Jeep and he was trying to remember where he'd set the control panel for the house.

"What are you looking for?" she asked.

"The controls."

"You'll move faster without me. I'll wait right here." She opened the door to the Jeep and kept it cracked.

"Hold on a quick second." He rushed inside, realizing he'd placed the control panel on the side table while helping Alyssa out to the Jeep. He armed the alarm and then set the timer to lock the door in thirty seconds. He left the control panel on the table and jetted out the door.

Alyssa was gone.

There'd been no screaming and he hadn't been inside for more than a minute. She wasn't in the Jeep.

He glanced up the road and saw brake lights. He bolted toward the driver's seat and was inside with the engine running in two shakes.

If the other vehicle got away, it was over. He knew it deep in the pit of his stomach. The vehicle was blacked out, no lights unless the driver tapped the brakes. It was a dark color, gray or black. The license plate had been removed. Following wasn't difficult considering the two-lane street was quiet and the car was moving at a steady clip without drawing too much attention by speeding.

Why did the car seem familiar?

Using voice commands, he told his cell to call 911.

"What's your emergency?" the dispatcher asked.

He identified himself as an officer and then explained the situation, giving a rapid-fire version.

"Stay on the line, sir. I have several officers in the area. One is a couple of blocks away."

"Can you have the officer block off Amethyst Road?"

"Hold on, please." She returned a few seconds later. "Affirmative."

The vehicle wouldn't get out of the neighborhood. A small win but he'd take it. Alyssa was somewhere in the vehicle. The thought of her in the trunk, cramping, trying to breathe was a gut punch. She could be in the back seat, hunkered over, he reasoned.

He pulled close enough to see eyes staring at him through the rearview mirror—eyes he recognized as Liz's.

"The person driving the vehicle in front of me is a fellow officer," he informed Dispatch. "Her name is Liz Roark and she should be considered armed and dangerous. She also has kidnapped a late-term pregnant woman and has her in her vehicle."

"Roger that."

His heart sank to the pit of his stomach. Alyssa would have been surprised but not shocked to see Liz pull up or come around the corner. Had she stopped by earlier to case the place? Check out the security situation. See if there were any holes or opportunities she could exploit?

Sirens sounded in the distance and Liz's eyes locked on to Blake's.

"Don't do this, Liz." He said the words out loud, hoping she could read his lips. Could he call her and talk her out of doing something she would regret?

Keeping the dispatcher on the line was the smart thing to do. It was protocol. But, dammit, he couldn't take a risk with Alyssa's life. With his child's life. There was a darkness to Liz's eyes, and he had no idea if he could get through to her. Not trying wasn't an option.

"I have to go," was all he said. He ended the call to the background noise of protests coming from the dispatcher. He used voice commands to call Liz.

She refused to answer.

So, he called again. He would keep calling until she picked up. His second call went straight to voice-mail. He flashed high beams at her and called again.

This time, she picked up.

"Don't do this, Liz," he warned. "Stop and let's talk this out."

"It's a little late for that, Blake."

"It's never too late to do the right thing," he said.

She issued a sharp sigh.

"A marked vehicle is on its way. Those sirens are coming for you. Let's stop and talk about a plan. I can help you."

"Why would you do that?" she scoffed. Her voice might be familiar but there was a detached quality that sent an icy chill racing down his back.

"We go back a long way, Liz."

"It's too late for me now." The distant quality had an air of hopelessness.

"Impossible. Whatever is going on, we can find a solution." He was careful not to make promises he knew would be impossible to keep. Like they could find a way out of this for her. There was no denying the fact she was in serious trouble.

"Right, O'Connor. And if I believe that I bet there's a bridge you want to sell me."

His logical appeal wasn't working. The sirens were getting closer. She had to know she was trapped. So, why was she so calm?

"Liz, stop the car."

"No, thanks."

"Please."

"I can't."

Can't? "Why not. You're the one in control here."

The throaty laugh she released was almost manic.

"Is that what you believe? That I'm the mastermind behind all this? I thought you knew me better than that, Blake."

"Then tell me." Questions were mounting but asking directly could be a mistake. Liz sounded like she was on the ledge, about to jump off. "I want to know. I care about what happens to you."

"All you care about is that slut who doesn't deserve you." She was all fire and bitterness now.

"That's not true. You and I have always been close. From the first day we partnered up, we clicked." It was true. They'd had a comradery he now realized ran a lot deeper than close friends on her side.

She didn't respond.

"Stop the vehicle, Liz. Let's talk this out. Whatever you've gotten into, we can find the exit."

She put an end to the call without replying. For a few tense seconds, he thought she might do just the opposite, press the pedal to the metal. But then, brake lights.

He exhaled the breath he'd been holding.

As the vehicle came to a complete stop, lights from a squad car lit up the night sky. Blake put his Jeep in park and bolted from the driver's seat.

Hands in the air, he approached the driver's side of her vehicle. He scanned the back seat and his gut clenched when there was no sign of Alyssa.

Liz's window came down. She had a gun in her right hand, holding it against the steering wheel.

"You'll figure it out sooner or later, so I might as well go ahead and tell you. I'm Bus Stop."

"Pop the trunk, Liz." He used as calm and steady a voice as he could. A steady panic twisted his gut in knots.

She pulled the lever as the squad car roared up, blocking her exit. She was boxed in between his Jeep and the squad car in front.

"Step out of your vehicle and put your hands where I can see 'em." The stern female voice blasted through a loudspeaker.

Liz seemed to take a long moment to contemplate her options. Then came a sharp sigh.

"I'm sorry, Blake." The trunk popped open and then Liz set her weapon on the passenger seat.

Hands in the air, Blake backtracked a few steps. The trunk was empty.

Liz was a decoy.

Blake spun her around and looked her dead in the eyes. "You have two seconds to tell me where she is and where they're going."

To his surprise, she did.

ALYSSA WAS ON her side, hands duct-taped behind her back at the wrists. A cramp brought her knees to her chest as she bounced around in the back seat of the SUV. The vehicle was speeding down the small road toward an unknown destination. The only thing keeping her alive in her estimation was the information she had, and now she realized the information must be evidence against the Judge.

Was it the payouts? There was no way cash could be traced. She would have to have some other physical evidence linking the Judge to the crime. She'd put two and two together after Liz showed up.

Surprisingly, there was no tape over her mouth. But then, they wanted her to talk. If she could remember what they wanted and where it was, she wouldn't hesitate at this point. She'd hand over any information in exchange for her freedom.

The driver was tall in stature and had on a black hoodie. That's all she knew. She wouldn't be able to pick him up out of a lineup if her life depended on it. The Judge? One of his henchmen?

Then, there was Liz. How could she do this to Blake?

Breathing through the next cramp was useless. She grunted as the pain gripped her.

"Hey, settle down back there," the driver said. Not a voice she recognized.

Had she met the Judge before?

She remembered a box. There was a box that looked like one of those library lending boxes people set up in neighborhoods to exchange books. There was a false panel on the side, and she slipped the envelope inside. The drop-off was at the end of a street near the border town of Laredo. She was supposed to drive there once a month, just like her father had.

Memories came crashing back. On his deathbed,

her father had told her about a video recording. He kept it at her apartment in case someone came looking in his. The thumb drive was taped inside the red toolbox he kept in her one-car garage.

Her father knew who Bus Stop was and that would have led to the Judge. Could Liz be the Judge? Alyssa didn't think so. The cop fit the bill as Bus Stop. Being stuffed in the trunk stirred a memory. She'd been leaving for work early in the morning when two strangers approached her at her car. In the next moment, a rag of some kind was suddenly over her nose and mouth. There was a tacky smell…something strong that she couldn't quite identify. And then she was picked up and placed inside a trunk. That was as much as she recalled. Part of her wondered if she was blocking out the traumatic experience.

A few minutes passed without a cramp. Alyssa faked one anyway, discreetly noticing the driver checked the rearview mirror. All she could see clearly were dark eyes. Brown, almost black. Nervous.

She played up the nonexistent cramp.

"Everything all right back there?" If he wasn't the Judge, he might be taking her to him. Or out to a field where he could shoot her and leave her for dead.

The thought fueled more drama on the fake cramps.

"Lady, are you okay?" He slowed the vehicle and then pulled to the side of the road.

"No. I'm not. I'm having a baby right now in the

back seat. I'm a high-risk pregnancy, and I'm guessing that if anything happens to me before you or your boss—" she stopped long enough to fake a cramp, this time screaming. "I'm guessing you'll be in real trouble if you can't deliver me in one piece. So, you need to get me to a hospital."

Nervous eyes seemed to be assessing her. She turned up the drama another notch and acted like she was trying not to scream again. She was sweaty from the actual contractions.

He threw the gearshift in Park as he blew out a sharp breath before throwing his left shoulder into the door to open it.

The vehicle was still running. Could she lock him out? It seemed like all anyone had to do was put a hand near the handle to get the doors to unlock. The option was out. He was tall and thin. Was he strong? Could he fight?

She glanced around, searching for anything she could use as a weapon. There was nothing on the floorboard, nothing in the seat except for her and she was taking up the entire thing.

So, that left nothing to use but her feet. She pulled up her knees as far as she could get them, coiling them like a spring. As the door opened and he looked in, she saw headlights coming from behind.

He stopped, resting his arm on the top of the door and casually leaning against it. She waited for the car to get a little closer before she kicked. Panic tightened her chest as she tried to slow her breathing.

When she could hear the other vehicle's engine and the lights blared through the rearview, she tightened the coil. As the vehicle moved to pass them, she unleashed the spring. Her foot connected with the center of his chest with enough force to knock him back a couple of steps. She heard the screech of brakes as she scrambled to sit up. Back against the opposite door, she managed to grab the handle. She pushed it open and then fell out of the SUV, landing hard on her backside.

All she could do at that point was roll onto her side to try to absorb some of the fall. The wind was knocked out of her. She struggled to catch her breath. And when she did, she filled her lungs full of air and then screamed.

Chapter Twenty-One

The crack of a bullet split the air.

Blake saw the shooter as the man scrambled around to the back of the SUV for cover. Blake slammed his foot on the gas pedal, wedging his Jeep in front of the other vehicle to effectively pin it in. Dispatch was on the line for the second time.

"Sir, it sounded like a shot was fired."

"Yes, ma'am." He performed a quick check and didn't see any blood, and then gave a quick rundown of the situation.

"The closest officer I have is ten minutes out. Can you hang in there, sir?"

"No choice. Send an EMT, possible woman in labor." He left Dispatch on the line as he grabbed his backup gun, a Sig Sauer P938. He exited the driver's side, coming around the front of the vehicle. He dropped down on his knees, searching for the shooter.

It was too dark to see that far, so he'd have to move blind. Leading with his weapon he rounded the front of the vehicle and immediately ducked when another shot fired his way.

One shooter.

Blake liked those odds. Since the SUV had temporary tags and a trigger-happy driver, Blake figured this was the person he was looking for. He surveyed the area, looking for Alyssa. She had to be here. The fact she was silent was so not good.

His heart jackhammered his ribs, battering him from the inside out.

"My name is Officer O'Connor. Put your weapon down where I can see it," he demanded, using his authoritative cop voice.

There was no response.

Blake moved around to the back of his Jeep based on a hunch. Yeah, the guy was trying to climb inside his SUV. He could back away and leave the scene. *Nope.*

"Freeze. Stop right there," Blake ordered.

Another shot fired at him.

Blake took aim, locked on to his target and fired. The guy's left shoulder flew back on impact. A look of shock darkened his features.

"I said freeze."

The perp started to lift his right hand but something from behind knocked into him. He dropped onto the asphalt. Standing behind him with a look of fierce determination and a heavy-looking rock was Alyssa. She stepped on his right wrist as Blake rushed over.

First, he disarmed the perp. Then he had Alyssa grab a spare pair of zip cuffs from the glove box. He could see her struggling as the welcome sounds of sirens filled the night air.

"How did you find me?" she asked, before bending over with a cramp. One hand on the SUV, the other cradled her bump. Based on her breathing, this was a hard one.

"Liz," he stated. Frustrated he had to sit on the perp, Blake offered soothing words. When her breathing slowed, she looked over at him. Her skin had paled.

"Can you sit inside the Jeep?"

She nodded and struggled on her way over, stopping twice to brace herself with one hand on a vehicle.

"Tell me your name," Blake instructed.

"Cameron James."

"Cameron James?" Blake parroted. He was a known leader of a human trafficking ring, a weapons smuggler, and Blake could add a few more items to the list. His operation spanned Texas, New Mexico, Arizona and across the border to Mexico. "Are you the Judge?"

"Judge and jury."

A squad car pulled up almost immediately followed by an ambulance. An officer flew out of his vehicle, weapon at the ready.

"Officer O'Connor here." He rattled off his badge number as he held his hands in the air so the officer could see them. "My pregnant wife is in my Jeep possibly going into premature labor."

The officer waved over a pair of EMTs, who zipped right past Blake. They weren't far from the hospital and that was one of the few positives coming out of this situation aside from the arrests being made tonight. He could only hope the baby would be okay. Despite having just days to get used to the idea of becoming a father, Blake was already forming an attachment to the kiddo. And he knew this because the thought of losing her practically gutted him.

What was it about facing loss that made people realize just how much they wanted something? And the realization included the baby's mother. Now that Blake realized why Alyssa left, the no-win situation she was in, he knew they belonged together. But there was a caveat. A deal breaker that needed to be out in the open if she felt the same way.

As the officer took over, Blake jumped up to standing and couldn't get to Alyssa fast enough. One of the EMTs took off toward the ambulance and his heart clenched. From this angle, all he could see was Alyssa curled up on her side. One of the EMTs was talking to her. His voice was too low for Blake to hear exactly what was being said.

The second EMT was already hustling back with a gurney. All Blake could do was step out of the way. It didn't take but a minute for her to be loaded up.

"Are you Blake O'Connor?" one of the EMTs asked.

"Yes."

"You want to follow us to the hospital or ride in the front?"

"I'll follow." He wanted to have his vehicle with him in case she was released tonight. Of course, it was probably just a hope. With Bus Stop and the Judge behind bars, he wanted to bring his wife home.

He barely got a look at her face as she was wheeled by him. Sheet white, his stress levels skyrocketed. All he could think about was how brave she'd been to do what she had. If she hadn't hit the perp in the back of the head, who knew where they'd be right now.

In a few seconds, he was behind the wheel and turning his Jeep around. The ambulance hauled to the hospital and that had him worried. His work as a police officer told him a fast ambulance was always a bad sign. He started imagining the worst. Had a bullet hit Alyssa?

Thinking back, he didn't remember seeing any blood.

Was she having a miscarriage? He couldn't even go there hypothetically in his mind.

The drive to the hospital seemed like it took forever. The ambulance diverted to the ER bay. He parked as close as he could without getting towed.

Watching as Alyssa was unloaded from the back and seeing a nurse running toward the glass door from inside the hospital wasn't helping to calm his nerves. He caught up to them and ran inside.

The nurse stopped at the doors marked Authorized Personnel Only. She put her hand up to stop him. "Sorry, sir. Are you her husband?"

"I am," he said with conviction.

"If you'll take a seat in the waiting room, someone will be with you shortly."

Blake thought about throwing his family name around for a hot second. In the end, he figured he could wait just like everyone else who had a loved one behind those doors. He nodded before turning toward the glass-enclosed lobby.

There was a coffee machine. For lack of anything better to do, he made a cup. Besides, it could end up being a long night and he had no plans to leave. Once he made coffee, he sent a text to his brothers in a group chat. He didn't prefer to communicate that way, but it was more efficient than reaching out to each one individually.

His cell blew up almost immediately with words of encouragement along with offers to show up. His brother Riggs said he was on his way. No questions asked. No request needed. He'd sit in the parking lot if Blake wanted to be left alone.

He realized he had three unread texts from Aaron.

News is all over the dept re: Liz.

Seriously messed up!

You okay?

Blake couldn't agree more. He responded with, At hospital. Talk later?

After returning his cell to his pocket, he spent the next half hour sipping coffee and pacing. Waiting was the worst. He'd rather be the one lying in a hospital bed. Knowing Alyssa was back there and not having any idea what was happening with her or the baby made him wish he had a punching bag. In fact, hospital waiting rooms should have workout equipment instead of chairs. He could go for a run on the treadmill about now to work off some of the tension stringing his muscles so tight it felt like they might snap.

A familiar face peeked into the waiting room... Aaron's. Blake made a beeline for his friend, meeting him halfway across the room. Aaron pulled him into a bear hug.

"I got here as fast as I could," Aaron said.

"You didn't have to come."

"Yeah, I did. How is she?"

"No idea." Blake shrugged his shoulders.

"No one's been by to tell you what's going on?"

"Not yet."

"I'm sure everything's okay. This is a great hospital. She's in the best possible hands," Aaron said.

Blake appreciated the words of support. He issued a sharp sigh. "I hope they're doing all right."

"For what it's worth, Liz is ready to talk. She wants a lighter sentence in return for testifying against Cameron James. She's saying he blackmailed her once he found out she was your partner. She'd gotten herself into some financial trouble that she'd been hiding. Word was about to get out and he needed her protection here in Houston. She made sure he was the one your ex-father-in-law dealt with when she did a little digging into his business. He was easy pickings and needed help. They believe your father-in-law videoed Liz at the drop as insurance. They knew he had something on them and once he died, it would come out."

"I can't believe someone I trusted could turn on me like that."

"She's the reason your wife left you. Liz saw it as a bonus. She thought she had a chance with you. But then you were like a lovesick puppy and she realized you'd never get over Alyssa," Aaron said.

"Liz needs to be locked behind bars for what she did. We're supposed to be the good guys," Blake said.

"Makes it ten times worse when one of ours goes down like this," Aaron agreed.

"Speaking of which, I'm resigning as soon as I can meet with my SO." Blake hadn't expected to share the news beforehand, but he didn't want Aaron to be blindsided. "My place is with my family on the ranch."

"You *are* part of the millionaire ranching family." Aaron laughed. "I knew it."

"I'm still me. And I hope you'll come visit the ranch sometime." Blake meant it.

"It won't be the same without you on the force. But you gotta do what makes you happy."

"Blake O'Connor." A doctor stepped in the room, looking for the person who answered to that name.

"I'm Blake." He crossed the room with Aaron on his heels.

"First of all, your wife is resting comfortably and the baby is fine. Both are doing well. However, we'd like to keep your wife overnight for observation."

"Whatever you think is best." Relief was a flood to dry planes. "Can I see her?"

"Technically visiting hours are over. Under the circumstances, we can make an exception."

Blake had no plans to leave the hospital. Whether that meant sleeping in this lobby or being in her room, Alyssa would not be alone through this. She'd gone through too much of her pregnancy without his support. There was no way he was allowing that to happen tonight.

"I'll take off." Aaron pulled Blake into another bear hug.

"Let's connect later. Play some ball before I move on."

"Deal."

The doctor led Blake down a series of hallways and into an elevator. The final hallway was short, and he definitely pulled some looks from nurses and attendants. The halls were dimly lit and quiet.

The doctor stopped in front of a door. "Based on

the look on your face, you're staying all night. One of the chairs should turn into a bed."

"Thank you."

Blake took a few steps inside the room. "Hey. Okay if I come inside?"

"Yes." Her voice sounded sleepy and it tugged at his heart strings.

"The doc said I could stay all night," he said, moving to her side. He pulled up a chair beside her so she could see the seriousness in his eyes. "If you want me here, I'd like to stay."

"Yes." Her answer came fast, encouraging him to say what else was on his mind.

He took her hand in his and drew circles in the palm.

"You're okay?" he asked.

"Better now that you're here." With her free hand, she rubbed her bump. "I have to say that I'm feeling incredibly lucky right now. She seems to be doing fine despite the events of the past week. You're here."

Her eyes welled with tears. He reached up and gently thumbed one off her cheek after it fell.

"I don't mean to get sentimental." Her cheeks flushed in the warm light.

"You don't have to hold anything back around me, Alyssa. In fact, I want to see all sides to you. Especially the ones that are hard to show."

She studied him for a long moment. "You mean that, don't you?"

"Every word." He took a deep breath, deciding to go all in. "The only time I've ever meant words more was the day I told you that I would love you for the rest of my life. I meant it on our wedding day, and I mean it now. I never stopped loving you, Alyssa."

More of those tears streaked her cheeks.

"Walking away from you was the hardest thing I've ever done in my life, Blake. I tried to find a way to tell you without involving you."

"That would have been impossible. We both know it."

"We do." She took in a breath before continuing. "It felt like an impossible situation and I didn't want to drag you through the mud or cause you to lose your job. On his deathbed, my father asked me to keep the family business running. I didn't feel like I could let him down. And yet, I let you down in the process. And now everything is a mess."

"Not anymore. The people responsible are going to jail for a very long time. Justice will be served. The baby is safely growing inside her mother. And most importantly, *you* are going to be just fine."

"I might be physically okay, but I'll never be fine again. Not with you in my life, Blake. I blew your trust." She dropped her gaze to the blanket. She was working the material between her thumb and forefinger.

"Every marriage has its ups and downs."

"Yes, but we're not married anymore."

He didn't respond. Instead, he got down on one knee. She didn't immediately look up, but when she did, her eyes were filled with something that looked a lot like guarded optimism with a little disbelief sprinkled in.

"Alyssa O'Connor. You are my soulmate. You never stopped being my 'one' person. The one I want to fall to pieces with in each other's arms." He searched her eyes and saw what had drawn him to her in the first place, the kind of soul he wanted to grow old beside. "If you'll have me, I'd like to marry my wife again."

He was rewarded with the warmest, most genuine smile.

"Yes, Blake. I'll marry you again. Nothing in my world is as right as when we're together. And I'll fall to pieces in your arms as long as we do it together."

"I love you, Alyssa."

"I never stopped loving you."

He stood up, leaned over and kissed her belly. The baby kicked and his heart stirred.

"Do you want to touch her?" Alyssa asked.

He nodded, marveling at how strong the little one was. Alyssa took his hand and placed it on her belly. He felt the second kick.

"I think someone approves of this marriage." Alyssa's smile literally reached all the way to his heart.

"Good. Because I plan to be the best father I can."

"You had an amazing role model in your father. I know you'll be the best dad this little bean could ever hope for."

Blake kissed his wife. He couldn't wait to take his family home.

Chapter Twenty-Two

Despite the beeps and the constant checks by the nursing staff, Alyssa had had the best night of sleep in months. Maybe it was the fact that Blake was there, holding her hand the entire time. Or the knowledge her family would be together after thinking for so long that it never would.

She had no idea how her in-laws would react to the news, to everything, but a knock on her door told her she was about to find out.

"Come in," she whispered.

Blake had nodded off and she didn't want to wake him. Too late. He shot up and held tighter to her hand.

"We have a visitor," she said. "It's okay."

Riggs peeked his head inside the door. "Did someone say it was okay to come in?"

"Yes." Blake rubbed his eyes after pushing up to standing. He met his brother halfway across the room and the two embraced, bringing back warm memories of belonging to a big family.

Would they accept her now after everything that happened? After how much she hurt Blake, would they be able to forgive her?

Her answer came swiftly when Riggs ate up the real estate between them in a few strides.

"It sure is good to see you," he said, reaching for a hug.

"I've missed every one of you guys more than you could ever know," she responded.

Blake moved beside his brother and put a hand on his shoulder. "She said yes."

For a serious guy, Riggs practically beamed. He'd laugh if he heard his smile described that way. "Welcome back to the family where you belong."

She wiped at a stray tear. This wasn't a tear of sadness. This was pure joy rolling down her cheek. "Thank you, Riggs. It means a lot to hear you say that."

He turned to his brother and gave another bear hug, this time with a round of congratulations afterward.

It was good to be going home.

"Everyone sends their love," Riggs said. He'd always been one of the quiet ones. Hearing him speak up now in support of Alyssa and making her feel welcome reminded her how incredible the family she'd married into was.

"I'm so sorry about your father. He was an amazing person," she said.

"We're all still trying to deal with it. Mom is

doing better, though. Having new life on the ranch is helping," he admitted.

"I heard about a few of your brothers settling down recently," she said.

His face twisted up like he'd just swallowed a jalapeño. His reaction made her laugh.

"Don't get me wrong, it's good for you and Blake. Great for my other brothers too. That's way down the road for me, if at all," he quickly countered. The saying *thou dost protest too much* came to mind. "Besides, no one could put up with me for long."

As far as excuses went, she wasn't buying his. "There's no reason to rush. Believe me, when you find the right one, you just know. Then all you have to be is smart enough to grab hold and not let go."

Blake came around to the side of the bed and took a seat next to Alyssa. He clasped their hands and told his brother to sit down and stay awhile. The baby kicked. Alyssa was beginning to believe it was her stamp of approval.

"Arizona," Cash said on the call to Blake. "I've tracked a decade's old kidnapping ring to a little town outside Tucson. Dad was onto them too. I know for a fact. I put the pieces together after studying some of his notes."

"Then, we'll head to Arizona." No brainer for Blake.

"You won't. You have a baby on the way, due anytime now."

Alyssa needed him. He had no plans to leave her

alone here at the home stretch of her pregnancy. She'd been home three days now, and he'd done everything he humanly could to make her comfortable. "I can work the investigation from home. Be your eyes and ears on the ground here. The kidnapping ring is connected to Katy Gulch. They'll come back. They might even still be here. We need resources at home in case they strike again."

"Someone already tried," Cash informed.

"And?"

"Late model black Mustang. Temporary plates. Tried to kidnap a kid who was in a bouncer in the backyard with the family dog while the mom ran inside for a minute to get the kid a snack."

"The tags were obviously bogus."

"Agreed." Cash hesitated for a long moment before saying, "It's good you're coming home, Blake. I think I can speak for everyone when I say how much we all miss you."

"The timing is finally right," he said. No matter how much he'd come to bond with his coworkers, no one could ever replace family. "And, Cash, I've missed the hell out of you guys too."

"We can't wait to welcome you and your family home, brother." Those were the only words Blake needed to hear. His wife and kid would be coming home to be with his family. And it was only a matter of time before they put an old ghost to rest.

* * * * *

Look for the next two books in
USA TODAY *bestselling author Barb Han's*
An O'Connor Family Mystery series
in November and December 2021.

And don't miss the previous books in the series:

Texas Kidnapping
Texas Target
Texas Law

Available now
wherever Harlequin Intrigue books are sold!

#2031 TEXAS STALKER
An O'Connor Family Mystery • by Barb Han

While fleeing an attempt on her life, Brianna Adair is reunited with her childhood friend Garrett O'Connor. Trusting others is not in her nature, but Brianna will have to lean on the gorgeous rancher or risk falling prey to a stalker who won't stop until she's dead...

#2032 STAY HIDDEN
Heartland Heroes • by Julie Anne Lindsey

Running from her abuser is Gina Ricci's only goal, and disappearing completely may be the answer. But local private investigator Cruz Winchester wants to arrest her ex and set Gina free. When everyone in Gina's life seems to become a target, will Cruz be able to save them all...without sacrificing Gina or her unborn child?

#2033 ROGUE CHRISTMAS OPERATION
Fugitive Heroes: Topaz Unit • by Juno Rushdan

Resolved to learn the truth of her sister's death, Hope Fischer travels to the mysterious military-controlled town where her sister worked at Christmas. Teaming up with the enigmatic Gage Graham could lead to the answers she's looking for—if Gage's secret past doesn't find and kill them first.

#2034 K-9 PATROL
Kansas City Crime Lab • by Julie Miller

After his best friend's sister, KCPD criminalist Lexi Callahan, is attacked at a crime scene, K-9 officer Aiden Murphy and partner Blue will do anything to protect her. But being assigned as her protection detail means spending every minute together. Can Aiden overcome his long-buried feelings for Lexi in time to save her from a killer?

#2035 FIND ME
by Cassie Miles

Searching for her childhood best friend requires undercover FBI agent Isabel "Angie" D'Angelo to infiltrate the Denver-based Lorenzo crime family. Standing in her way is Julian Parisi, a gentleman's club manager working for the Lorenzo family. Angie will need to convince Julian to help even though she knows he's got secrets of his own...

#2036 DEADLY DAYS OF CHRISTMAS
by Carla Cassidy

Still recovering from a previous heartbreak, Sheriff Mac McKnight avoids Christmas at any cost, even with his deputy, Callie Stevens, who loves the holidays—and him. But when a serial killer's victims start mirroring *The Twelve Days of Christmas*, he'll have to confront his past...and his desire for Callie.

"So, tell me who you *think* is stalking you," he said in more of a statement than a question.

She shrugged her shoulders. "I don't know. That's a tough one. There's a guy in one of my classes who creeps me out. I'll be taking notes furiously in class only to get a weird feeling like I'm being watched and then look up to see him staring at me intensely."

"Has he come around the bar?"

"A time or two," she admitted.

"Is he alone?"

"As far as I can tell. He never has worked up the courage to come talk to me, so he takes a table by the dance floor and nurses a beer," she said.

"Any idea what his name is?"

"Derk Waters, I think. I overheard someone say that in a group project when his team was next to mine. By the way, there should be no group projects in college. I end up doing all the work and have to hear complaints from everyone in the process," she said as an aside.

Garrett chuckled. "Maybe you should learn to let others pull their own weight."

She blew out a sharp breath. "And risk a failing grade? No, thanks. Besides, I tried that once and ended up staying up all night to redo someone's work because they slapped their part together."

"Sounds like something you'd do," Garrett said.

"What's that supposed to mean?" She heard the defensiveness in her own voice, but it was too late to reel it in.

"You always were the take-charge type. I'm not surprised you'd pull out a win in a terrible situation."

Well, she really had overreacted. She exhaled, trying to release some of the tension she'd been holding in her shoulders. "Thanks for the compliment, Garrett. It means a lot coming from you. I mean, your opinion matters to me."

"No problem." He shrugged off her comment, but she could see that it meant something to him, too. He picked up his coffee cup and took another sip. "Okay, so we have one creep on the list. What about others?"

"I wouldn't classify this guy as a creep necessarily, but he has followed me out to the parking lot at school more than once. He's a TA, so basically a grad student working for one of my professors. He made it known that he'd be willing to help if I fell behind in class," she said.

Again, that jaw muscle clenched.

"Doesn't he take a hint?"

"Honestly, he's harmless. The only reason I brought him up was because we were talking about school and for some reason he popped into my mind. He's working his way through school and I doubt he'd risk his future if he got caught," she surmised. "Plus, this person is trying to run me off the road."

"You rejected him. That could anger a certain personality type," he said. "What's his name?"

"Blaine something. I don't remember his last name." Up to this point, she hadn't really believed the slimeball could be someone she knew. A cold shiver raced down her spine at the thought. "I've been working under the assumption one of the guys at the bar meant to get a little too friendly."

"We have to start somewhere. I believe my brothers would say the most likely culprit is someone you know. I've heard them say a woman's biggest physical threat is from those closest to her. Boyfriend. Spouse. Someone in her circle." He shot a look of apology. "It's an awful truth."

She issued a sharp sigh. "I can't even imagine who would want to hurt me."

Don't miss
Texas Stalker *by Barb Han,*
available November 2021 wherever
Harlequin Intrigue books and ebooks are sold.

Harlequin.com

HIEXP1021